The Story of Jack

The Pit Bull Who Became a Hero

PAM DAOUST

For all the Good Dogs

Especially the Pit Bulls
Who often get an undeserved Bad Rap…
…And especially for Gigi, Nina, Gus and Maddy,
Who Take Such Good Care of their Humans.

~

"A powerful story…beautiful and uplifting."
~ Sara Hoklotubbe, award-winning author of SINKING SUSPICIONS

CONTENTS

Prologue

Hero is a Human word usually accompanied by lots of praise and a pat on the head.

I'd rather have a piece of bacon.

Crunchy, salty and smelling so irresistibly delicious that I slobber on myself just thinking of it, bacon is a Special Treat that I don't get nearly enough of. This seems to be true of so many things I like to gobble down fast. When it's gone, I'm left with only a memory that makes me lick my chops in longing.

Of course, being a dog, I love adoring pats on the head, but I don't dwell on the things that happened that make Humans think I'm a Hero. It's not my nature to dwell on things—except perhaps for Special Treats like bacon.

Yet I seem to be doing a lot of "dwelling in the past" lately and I don't know why, or what it all means.

Perhaps becoming a Hero has made me feel Important. Or maybe I've just always felt *Important*—as if My Life matters. Every single one of my past experiences has felt as if it *really* mattered; there was some reason for it. And all of those experiences combined together make up this thing called My Life.

It could be that *every*one just feels this way—but maybe not. I'm no expert on such things. After all, I *am* just a dog when all is said and done.

Still, I've been told that I'm Special. Unique. However, I find myself wondering if that's not true of every single living creature—Human or Otherwise— that I've ever met. Looking back, they all seem Special and Unique to me. (Even cats—but don't tell anyone I said so.)

No two are alike certainly. In telling *my* story, I'll also be telling *their* stories. They are every bit as Important as I am. Some are Heroes in their own right. It's just that no one knows about them. If I'm a Hero, so are they. We are all connected, anyway, through mutual experience if nothing else…

Granted, it's a bit Presumptuous of me to think I know best how to tell someone else's story when they can very well tell their own. If they want to, that is. Not everyone *wants* to tell their story, especially if they are embarrassed by it. And I've met a few Bad Sorts who *should* be embarrassed.

"Presumptuous" is another Human word that's been applied to me on occasion—when I help myself to a Human's roast beef right off his plate, for example. My only excuse is that the Human in question never should have set his piled-high with yummy roast beef plate at nose level on the coffee table right in front of me and then gone to get something in the kitchen.

I was lucky that time. Since I was still in the Recent Hero stage, no one even *thought* to scold me—but I did get some Quelling Looks and resolved to mend my thieving ways at once…. Don't want to disappoint. I have an image to maintain, after all.

And that brings me round again to the idea of finally telling My Story. My *Whole* Story. No one really knows it but me. There are those who *think* they know me, and those who *do* know me quite well actually, but no one *really* knows me. Not all of me, anyway. Hero or Villain, I am not what People call me. Or how they think of me. Or even how I think of myself, since that changes from day to day.

What I am is a Being made up of *all* my previous experiences—and I do mean *all*. And it is all those experiences that led—somehow—to my being in the right place at the right time to become a Hero just when a Hero was needed.

I know this sounds confusing; I'm still trying to sort it out myself.

What I'm hoping is that when I get to the end of telling My Story, everything will suddenly become clear. I will know the meaning of Life—or at least of *My* Life. I've been chasing that particular tennis ball for about as long as I can remember. Just when I think I've gotten all the mysteries and uncertainties figured out, something happens to take me to a whole new place, where I have to start all over again, *figuring things out.*

I don't want that to happen this time if I can help it. I quite like where I am. And I want to remember everything I've learned, especially the lessons I don't want to repeat.

So I think I should just start recollecting My Story and then make of it what I must. I've spent my whole Life listening to Everyone Else. Now, at long last, is *my* time to Speak. And Speak I finally will.

Woof!

Is anyone out there listening?

CHAPTER ONE

The Beginning

My Story begins simply. I came into a world about which I knew *nothing*—not that any of us knows much about The World before we get here. We learn as we go. And the first thing I learned is that "Coming Into The World" is a risky business. Even in the best of circumstances, it's messy and uncomfortable. My own birth was more stressful than I had expected. The only reason I agreed to go through with it in the first place is because I had no more room where I was. It was so crowded I could not turn around anymore.

Five of us were competing for what little space could be found—five puppies. Pit Bulls, I later learned we were called, but at the time, I did not know what we were.

I only knew that we *were*…five of us—squirming and fighting and pushing against each other in far too small of a space. Then, right before I was born, I was squeezed half to death. I mean, *really* squeezed.

I was so relieved to have the squeezing stop that I did not mind getting dumped into the cold, though I must say that the sudden change in temperature came as a rude shock.

I was one of the first ones out and I knew—without knowing how I knew—that I needed warmth or I would die. It would be over before it had barely started.

It took all my strength to crawl over to my mother and huddle against her warm body and welcoming fur. She licked me all over and seemed very glad to see me. Her tongue felt warm and scratchy on my back—her nose cold and wet. I loved the smell of her—so rich and comforting. I could not see her yet, as my eyes were tightly shut. Indeed, I did not know I had eyes at this point in my life, but I knew my mother was nearby and that I needed to be close to her—as close as I could possibly get.

The rest of my brothers and sisters came soon after me, and there we were, all five of us trying to get warm against my mother—and searching for something to eat—something to restore us after the hard work of being dumped into a strange, cold world.

When you are a puppy born in an alley on a freezing winter day, eating is The Most Important Thing. Even in the best of circumstances, puppies need to eat as soon as possible—or they will soon weaken and die.

I knew that. No one had to tell me.

For some reason, I was bigger and stronger than my brothers and sisters.

I was meant to succeed.

Being bigger and stronger meant that I could keep my place near my mother when my siblings tried to push me out of the way. I stayed right where I was and drank my mother's warm milk. It kept me alive through the long freezing night.

I drank her sweet milk and snoozed. Awoke and drank again.

When morning came and the warmth found us, I did a little nosing around myself and realized that the warmth—or sunshine, as I later learned it was called—had shown up too late.

Three of my siblings were still and cold. The fourth was barely alive.

"Come here," I called to that fourth small sibling.

Swept with a feeling that I did not then know was called Compassion, I wanted to help. Later, I was to learn that Compassion is essential, not only to my own survival but to the survival of just about every other species on earth. "Come on," I urged in my squeaky, thin voice. "Drink some milk. You'll feel better if you do."

The pup sighed, her voice barely a whimper. No matter about her voice. Her thoughts were easy to understand. They just came to me without much effort on my part—or hers.

"It's too late for me," she answered quite clearly. "You drink the milk. I have to Go Back To Where I Came From."

I tried to remember That Other Place—the place I had come from. Already it was a distant memory of warm sunny days, beautiful green fields to run in, clear running water and a feeling of Being Loved…. Being Loved with a Love So Big that it covered all the universe and everything in it…. Most especially including me.

I knew I would never really forget that place—or the feeling of Being Loved. But already, the details were a little hazy. I only knew that I had agreed to come here for some Purpose, some Great Lofty Purpose.

But, now that I was here, I had forgotten what it was.

My first task—my biggest job—was going to be to remember. To rediscover that Purpose and live it out as best I could. After all, isn't that all any of us are meant to do when we suddenly show up here?

Starting the very minute I was born, I devoted myself to discovering My Purpose, My Reason For Being Here…wherever *here* actually was. At this point in my life, even that was unclear to me.

But my first job, it soon became apparent, was to *Survive.*

So I spent the day sleeping and drinking my mother's sweet milk—and trying to stay warm.

My mother's sadness at losing her other babies surrounded me. She nosed them and licked them—especially the weak one who still lived. But that night, when the cold came, the girl pup—my sister—died.

My mother whimp   l and licked her. "Don't go," she pleaded. "Little One, don't go yet!"

But it was too late. My sister had already gone.

The Warmth and Cold came two more times, and I could feel my mother getting weaker. She herself needed to eat and drink, but she would not leave me or my siblings, even though they were no longer "with us."

My mother was a good, brave mother. The best. She was doing all she could, which—I was to discover—is all any of us can do when faced with Insurmountable Problems. We must do The Best We Can.

At night, I could feel her shivering from her nose right down to the tip of her tail.

Crawling almost underneath her, I myself was fairly warm. The concrete on which I lay was cold and hard, but the warmth of my mother's body kept me alive.

Then, on the morning of the third day, just as the sun found us again, I heard a voice. The first Human voice I had ever heard.

"Mom! Mom, look. Look what I found."

"Oh, no," another voice said. "That's so sad. That poor dog had her puppies right here in the alley and it looks as if most of them didn't make it."

"But one of them did, Mom. The brown one is still alive. Can we take them home with us? Can we keep them? I'll take care of them. I've got a paper route now; that's enough money to feed them."

"No, Tim. I'm sorry. We can't afford one dog, let alone two. Besides, you and I are gone most of the day. You at school…me at work…. If your Dad were still alive, it might be different. I'd still be home during the day to look after them, the way I was when you were small."

"But, *Mom!*"

"No buts, Tim. This isn't a breed I would want for a pet, anyway. These look like Pit Bulls—at least, the Mom does. From what I've heard, Pit Bulls are dangerous, aggressive dogs bred for fighting. They say you never can trust one. Unlike other dogs, they could turn on you in a heartbeat."

"They don't look very dangerous to me."

Doubt and uncertainty laced Tim's tone. I had to agree with him. Was I dangerous? Was my shivering, half-starved mother aggressive? Where did these ideas come from, anyway? Who decided these things without even a word of discussion on the matter?

Humans have all sorts of Strange Ideas that a dog can scarcely comprehend. Much of what Humans do is downright baffling and makes no sense whatsoever to us canines. I mean I know we all come from the Same Place—That Other Place—but other than that, we don't have much in common, do we?

All I wanted was to be warm and safe and to have enough to eat. If I had all that, I would be so Grateful. I would spend all my days taking care of whoever took care of me. I would be loyal and stand by them and do whatever I could to please them. I would never bite or betray them. Young as I was, blind as I was, just born as I was, I *knew* these things. I knew them with a certainty as real as the cold surrounding me, and the sunlight teasing me with its warmth.

But I was just a pup back then and the world and the Humans in it were still a mystery to me. I was just a pup who would die in an alley along with my brothers and sisters and probably also my mother. Another cold night without sunshine should do it.

"Mom," said Tim. "We can't just leave them here. We have to *do* something."

"But we're already late, Tim. We have so much to do today. We can't take time to..."

"*Please,* Mom? Please, can't we do something for them? They'll die if we just leave them here. It's so cold. And it's supposed to snow tonight. That's what the weatherman said. He said we might not have school tomorrow."

There came a long sigh. A pause. The very air turned expectant, as if it were waiting for something. Waiting to decide my fate. Waiting to decide if I, too, was meant to Go Back To Where I Came From...before I had lived My Purpose or learned about this strange new place in which I now found myself.

"Oh, all right. Run and get a couple of big bath towels and...and a laundry basket. If we can get them into the car...if the mother dog doesn't try to bite us...we'll take them to the Animal Shelter. Get them out of the cold, anyway. What happens to them after that is the Shelter's problem. We'll have done all we can, Tim. Maybe someone who knows about this kind of dog will adopt one or both of them."

"Sure. Great! I'll go get the towels and the laundry basket."

And that was how my mother and I wound up at the Animal Shelter.

CHAPTER TWO

The Animal Shelter

When I think of Animal Shelters, I think of Cages. A Cage is where they put you where you can't get out. You have to stay there. You can't go anywhere else. You have no choice but to live, day after day, inside that place—the Cage.

The Animal Shelter had *lots* of cages. And in that part of the building where my mother and I were taken, the Cages were full of dogs, all kinds of dogs.

Big dogs. Small dogs. Old dogs. Young dogs. Each of them stuck inside a Cage with no way to get out unless someone came along and opened the door to their particular Cage.

We were given water to drink and food twice a day. The food was called Kibble and it made a plunking sound and rolled around a little when it was poured into my mother's feed pan.

I was still too small to be much interested in Kibble, which did not seem too terribly appetizing, even though it had an interesting smell. I had my mother and her warm milk. I figured that was all I needed.

I still could not see much that was happening around me—but I could hear and smell. In the way that *all* animals have of knowing, I knew what was going on in My World. I had Good Instincts.

My mother cringed away from the Humans who came to look at us. The Humans who had first put us into the Cage—the Shelter Workers—came and looked at us everyday. They sometimes opened the cage and reached inside it to pet my mother. But my mother was having none of it.

She did not bite. She did not growl. She was too kind and gentle for that. But, she was afraid. Whatever her experiences had been with Humans, she did not trust them one bit. So she cowered in the back of the Cage and tried to protect me as best she could by crowding me into the cramped space behind her.

"This Mama dog won't be a good candidate for adoption," one of the Shelter Workers said. "She's afraid of People. Poor thing. And of course, her breed will always be working against her. She's definitely got some Pit Bull in her."

"But the pup will be cute when it gets bigger," the other Worker answered. "We can probably find a home for the pup. Even if he *is* a Pit Bull. Puppies are so sweet, after all."

"Yes, but it means keeping both of them a lot longer—until the pup can be weaned. And we're so crowded. New dogs are coming in every day. We don't have enough space for all of them."

"Oh, but surely we can save the pup, at least. Once the little guy is weaned, it shouldn't take long to find him a home. All we need is the Right Person."

"Hmmmmm…. But, what if we don't find the Right Person? Seems to me it would be best to take them *both* down the hall right now and be done with it."

Down The Hall.

I had no idea what *that* meant. But I knew it meant Something Bad and so did my mother. My mother was trembling. She was shaking from nose to tail at the very mention of going Down The Hall.

After the Shelter Workers left, I asked my mother what Down The Hall meant.

"I don't know," my mother whispered. "But I have seen the Shelter Workers take other dogs—and cats, too—Down The Hall. There's a big door at the end of the hallway. And once the dogs and cats go through that doorway and the door closes, they never come out again."

Uh, oh. That did not sound good. I could feel my mother's fear. It was like a physical presence all around me. It became a part of me. Small as I was, half-blind as I still was, I began to take notice—and sure enough, every single day, the Shelter Workers took dogs and cats Down The Hall.

Lots of them.

And they were never seen again.

At the other end of the hallway was another door—but this door was usually open. People—Humans—came in and out of that doorway all day long.

And somewhere, in another part of this building, was a place where the cats were kept. Sometimes, I could hear them meowing and crying their awful cat cries. I was curious about cats and the noises they made, but I did not much like those particular sounds. I much preferred a good, solid "woof!" to those mewling cat sounds—and I still do, today.

Young as I was, I knew that cats were different from me—and they always seemed to be complaining. When the Shelter Workers carried cats Down The Hall past us dogs, the cats were often in cat carriers, whereas the dogs were usually led at the end of a line—a leash, it was called—held by the Shelter Worker.

Sometimes, if they—the dogs—were too weak and sick to walk—and many were—they were carried.

I could always smell the fear of the cats and dogs being taken Down The Hall. Somehow they knew—just as I did—that they would not be coming this way again.

The Animal Shelter was not a happy place.

Normally, I was not one to think much about the future—or to worry about it. But I myself began to be very afraid about the possibility of being taken Down The Hall.

Still, there were Bright Moments in the Animal Shelter.

Humans came everyu.. to peer inside the Cages and look long and hard at us dogs—and, I presume, the cats at the other end of the building.

They would coo at us and talk to us and sometimes even bang a little on our Cages or stick their fingers inside and wiggle them at us.

My mother would cringe in the back of the Cage, but as I got bigger, I took an interest and wanted to investigate these activities. I was curious and wanted to know more about the world and these beings called People or Humans.

Actually, I liked them. They smelled interesting. I wanted to play with them. I wanted to play with anyone and anything that I saw. I wanted to run and jump and tumble. I knew I would get stronger if I did all these things. It was my nature to be curious and to investigate and to be interested in just about Everything.

My mother was *not* much interested. She played a little at times—but mostly, she didn't. There was no room to really run and jump and do all the things I wanted to do.

I would sniff at the fingers stuck through the wire mesh of our Cage. Sometimes, I would even lick them.

"Oh, this puppy is so cute! Can I adopt this puppy?" People sometimes asked.

The answer was always the same. "Not yet—but soon. Once the puppy is weaned. And he'll need to be neutered and have all his shots first. *Then* we will allow him to be adopted. If you don't find another dog today, come back when he's ready."

Each day I grew bigger and stronger. I started to look more like myself—the way I would look when I got bigger. I was no longer just any old puppy, with a puppy's general cuteness. To most folks, all puppies look alike—cute and small. But it soon began to become apparent that I was indeed a Pit Bull puppy. Whatever a Pit Bull is that makes it different from other dogs.

I also started to take an interest in the food they gave to my mother. It smelled more and more worthy of inspection. Soon, I was eating Kibble right alongside my mother—and my eyesight had improved so much that I could see everything I wanted to see.

Not that there was all that much to see inside our Cage or the Animal Shelter itself

Still, there were those Bright Moments.

Sometimes, People came, chose a dog from one of the Cages and left—taking the dog with them. These were the Happy Moments—moments every dog wanted to have.

We all knew that the chosen dogs had found Someone Special—A Forever Friend. We knew that they had found something called Love.

Inexperienced as I still was about almost everything, I knew that Love was The Most Important Thing—the thing that is needed by *all* living creatures—even cats.

Some memory of Being Loved somewhere, *some* time, still stayed with me though I could recall none of the details—and in fact, was most eager to learn more about it. To *re*-experience it. Love had something to do with that *other* big thing—My Purpose, my reason for having come here to begin with. Both were mixed up in my mind and not something I even thought about much. I was still a puppy, after all, and had little notion—and less inclination—to ponder things that seemed so confusing and so much bigger than me.

What I *did* know was that when a dog was *chosen* at the shelter, it meant that it was *Loved*. Or at least, it was *going* to be Loved. That was the plan, anyway. That's the way it looked to me when Humans made a big fuss over a dog and then took it away with them.

Sometimes, I'm sorry to say, a Human would bring a dog back again, complaining that it was not the right dog for them. When that happened, the dog almost always ended up being taken Down The Hall. There were just too many dogs to allow for second chances.

Even given the terrible uncertainty that things might not work out in the end, all the dogs got excited when a New Prospect appeared. A New Prospect was a Person who wanted a dog for his or her very own. This was a Person who came to the Animal Shelter to choose a dog and take it away with him or her.

The Person would walk up and down the aisle of Cages, look inside each one, and then make a choice. Sometimes, the Person agonized over that choice. Sometimes, he or she seemed to know right away which dog was the Perfect One.

During this selection process, some of the dogs barked and leapt at the doors of their Cages, all of them woofing, "Take me! Take me! I'm the dog for you. Please get me out of here. Hurry. I need Someone. Take me home before they come and take me Down The Hall!"

I loved the excitement and the happy feeling all of us got whenever a New Prospect came to check us out. This was a chance to leave our Cages forever and go wherever some Friendly Person wanted to take us. It was a chance for a new life, a new love, a happily ever after. And maybe, if we were lucky, Special Treats, too.

Anyplace seemed better than the Animal Shelter and the dark threat of having to go Down The Hall because we had *not* been chosen.

Then came the day when the Shelter Workers came to our Cage and looked inside at my mother and me. Their faces were very serious, as Human faces are apt to get when their owners are thinking Serious Thoughts.

I could feel their energy, and I was suddenly afraid—very afraid.

So was my mother.

She cringed as she always did and told me to come hide behind her.

I wanted to play so I ignored the command. I thought if I played with these People, maybe their energy would change, and they would not be so sad and serious. Maybe they would stop thinking Serious Thoughts.

I pranced and danced, ignoring my mother's warnings, but nothing I did seemed to change anything. Their energy remained dark and threatening.

"It's time for Mama to go Down The Hall," said one of the two Shelter Workers watching us. "I hate to do it, but it's time."

"Yes, I'm afraid it is. The pup is healthy and strong—ready to be on his own now. Ready for us to find him a new home. If we can, that is."

"We were right about that poor Mama never being able to find a home. Just look at her. She may not be so starved-looking as when she first came in here, but she just doesn't have the Right Attitude for adoption. She'll always be scared and cowering. Even if someone was willing to take her, she might not make it in the outside world. Given enough provocation, she still might become Aggressive and Dangerous. It's a shame but we can't risk it with a dog of this breed. Placing a Pit Bull is always a gamble, isn't it, especially older ones whose background we know nothing about?"

"Then let's get it over with. I'll get a leash."

And that was how I lost my mother.

I cried and cried and jumped all over protesting when they took her away, but she was taken Down The Hall—dragged at the end of a leash, whimpering as she called out her goodbyes to me. She dug in with her feet and fought, trying to slip her collar—but they just dragged her away... and I never saw her again.

CHAPTER THREE

Life Without My Mother

Time passed as I grieved for my mother and tried to get used to living Life without her.

The Shelter Workers did unpleasant things to me; they gave me sharp pokes with something they called a "shot", putting me to sleep and then, when I woke up, leaving me hurting, sad and feeling very much alone in my Cage.

After they did these unpleasant things, they did try and comfort me. Sometimes, they took me out of my Cage and played with me. Those were the best times I had in the Animal Shelter. When the Shelter Workers laughed and played with me, tossing me a red squeaky toy that I could pounce on and chew, they made me forget about the sad times, like losing my mother.

I simply was not made to hold a grudge—or to be sad for long.

Life was waiting to be lived!

I, too, began to watch for my chance with a New Prospect.

Like the other dogs, I learned to whine, wag my tail, jump up and cling to the mesh of my Cage, and generally demand attention whenever New Prospects came to check out us dogs.

"What kind of dog is that?" a Human female asked one day, as she stuck a finger inside my Cage to scratch me under the chin. The corners of her mouth were turned up and she had a nice energy—nothing dark about her that I could sense.

I wiggled all over and licked her finger, telling her in no uncertain terms that I was the Perfect Dog for her.

"Oh, that's a Pit Bull puppy."

"A Pit Bull!" The woman jerked her hand away from me and stepped back from my Cage. Her energy changed in an instant as the corners of her mouth drew downward. "You're adopting out Pit Bulls? That's a dangerous breed. This pup should be put down, not adopted out to some unsuspecting family."

"Under the right circumstances, a Pit Bull can make a very good pet," defended the Shelter Worker. "While it's true that I've seen some Bad Ones, they were ruined by Bad Owners. I've also seen some very Good Ones, so you shouldn't judge them harshly just because of their breeding."

Her eyes sparked a little with a hint of some dark emotion, but I knew her to be kind to *me*, even if she *had* helped to take my mother Down The Hall. (She also was someone who liked to toss the squeaky toy to me.) I was pleased to hear her defending the kind of dog I was—the *breed* I was.

"Not in *my* book there are no Good Ones. Haven't you heard the stories about how vicious they can be? Pit Bulls should be banned—and they're talking about doing just that. These dogs are born killers. You can never trust one. In absolutely no circumstances should they be adopted out."

"I'm sorry, but I have to disagree with you. Just look at this little fellow. He's like any *other* puppy—happy and eager to please. Given the right training, the right discipline and lots of love…"

"Nonsense. No training in the world can overcome breeding and basic tendencies. If this is the kind of place you run here, I'll choose a puppy from somewhere else."

"But, we have lots of other dogs who need homes—dogs who *aren't* Pit Bulls. Won't you at least take a look at them?"

"Not if you can't do a better job of screening dogs put up for adoption. You're trying to foist off Pit Bulls as suitable pets, and no way can I approve of that. I'll take my business elsewhere, thank you very much."

After the Woman left, I sat down in my Cage and thought about all I had heard. Why was it so bad to be a Pit Bull? I would never hurt anyone. Yet no one really seemed to like or trust Pit Bulls. I just wanted a home and someone to Love me. I wanted to get out into the world and see things, go places and find out what My Purpose was. I wanted Someone Special of my own to Love and take care of. That's all I wanted…. Was that so bad?

Later that day, two of the Shelter Workers—including the one I knew so well by now—came and stood looking down at me, and shaking their heads. Their energy felt very sad to me and I wished I could make them smile.

"I thought sure this little one would be gone by now. He's so cute. You'd think someone would be willing to give him a chance."

"He's a Pit Bull. That's two strikes against him right there. If the City passes that ordinance banning 'dangerous breeds' that everyone is talking about, he won't be adoptable, anyway…. Even as it is, he needs just the right owner who will take the time to Love and train him, so he will always be a good dog—a dog you can trust."

A Good Dog.

Yes, that's what I intended to be—a Good Dog. I would try so hard to be a Good Dog to any one who would adopt me. I did not understand the rest of what they were talking about, but I understood the idea of being a Good Dog.

And that's the kind of dog I would always be. Maybe not perfect— but *Good*. If I could not be perfect because I had been born a Pit Bull, at least I could be Good. I would *never* hurt anyone. That seemed to be what everyone was worried most about, that I would hurt someone. But what could make me *want* to hurt someone? All I wanted was Love.

"Well, we'll give him another week. If he's not gone by then, we'll have to take him Down The Hall. We have no choice. There are just too many other dogs who need a chance at adoption."

Oh, no! I flopped down in my Cage and rested my nose on my two front paws. This was so unfair. This was so…scary. I hadn't had time to live my life yet and Humans were talking about…about…

I did not want to think about what going Down The Hall meant. It wasn't something good and it wasn't something I wanted to happen. Not to *me*, anyway. Well, not to *anyone*. All I had to do was remember my mother going Down The Hall and I myself shook from nose to tail. But what could I do? How could I stop it from happening to me?

Whatever *it* was.

Darkness and light came—and then came again and again, and still, no New Prospect wanted me. Instead, I heard things like:

"Well, he's cute, but he *is* a Pit Bull. And I just can't take on a Pit Bull."

"How big will he get? Won't he become vicious as he gets older?"

"Hey, cool—is that one of them fighting dogs? Will he bite off my finger if I stick it into his Cage? What's he doing here? Isn't it against the law to keep Pit Bulls? If it isn't, it probably *should* be."

People looked. And People left. With other dogs. I wagged my tail as hard as I could and smiled at them, but they did not want to adopt me. Some folks seemed so afraid of me—of *me*. Which was clearly absurd.

Each day, I became more and more afraid. How long did I have before the Shelter Workers came and took me Down The Hall?

One afternoon, just before the Shelter closed for the day, the two Shelter Workers again came and looked at me. Their energy was really sad. So sad their mouths were drooping downward and I felt afraid to look into the eyes looking down at me.

"Tomorrow," one said. "Tomorrow, we'll have to take him Down The Hall. We need his Cage. It's too bad but no one wants a Rottweiler or a Pit Bull right now—not after all the fuss about dangerous breeds that we've been hearing lately. Even a sweet little guy like this one doesn't stand a chance."

"I know. I'd take him myself if only I had room. But I already have two dogs and a cat. Can't save them all. This poor little fella was doomed from the start."

They turned off the lights then and left. Left me alone and shivering with dread.

All that night, I shivered. I was so afraid and felt so alone that in the middle of the dark time, I began to bark. I barked and barked. I howled and cried.

"Shut up, will you?" growled the dog next door to me. "You're keeping me awake."

"But tomorrow, they're taking me Down The Hall!" I cried. "I heard them talking."

"Good. Then maybe tomorrow night I can get some sleep."

"But it's so unfair. Why won't anyone adopt me? I'll be a Good Dog."

"All of us in here would be Good Dogs if we had a chance. It's just the way of things. We're only dogs. Humans can do whatever they want with us. Same with cats. They can do whatever they want with cats, too—but then, who really cares about cats? Not me, certainly. I never have liked cats."

"But I don't want to go Down The Hall! I want to *live* first. I want to know Love. I want to have a Best Friend. I want to *be* a Best Friend."

"So do we all," said the Next Door Dog. "Don't think so much. It's better if you don't think so much. Can't change things, anyway. Haven't you learned that yet? You're just a dog. It's Humans who run the world. Humans make *all* the decisions."

I spent the rest of the Dark Time thinking about what he had said. He was right. So terribly right. I was thinking too much. Worrying and wondering. I could not change anything, so why did I bother? What would happen would happen.

Would it hurt, I wondered? Going Back To The Place I had Come From?

For that was what was going to happen. I was sure of it. Sometimes, when the door at the end of the hallway opened as a Shelter Worker and a dog entered. and then disappeared, the door closing behind them, I caught a whiff of something. Whatever it was struck terror into my bones and I would tremble just like my mother. My mother had been shaking so badly that she could hardly walk or keep fighting when they dragged her Down The Hall.

When she wasn't calling for me, she had been whimpering deep in her throat. I would probably whimper, too. I didn't know if I could help it. Maybe that's just what you do when you're Going Back to Where You Came From. Even if where you came from is a wonderful place but you just can't remember how wonderful it really is or was.

Morning came. The Shelter Workers arrived and turned on the lights. People started to come through the open door to look at us dogs.

Everyone started jumping and barking—calling for attention. But I just sat there. Too afraid, too certain I would not be chosen. I was a Pit Bull, after all. No one wanted me.

The Shelter Worker came and stood outside my Cage. She had a leash and a collar in her hand. I knew what that meant. She sighed. "Maybe I'll just wait until this afternoon. I won't do it this morning. I'll wait until after lunch, anyway. Or better yet, 'til just before I go home. This is your last day, little guy. You better get up and sell yourself. You only have a few more hours."

What can I do? I thought. How do I "sell myself"?

A man came up to my Cage and looked in at me. I wiggled my backside and smiled at him. I jumped up and down, frantic for his attention.

"Well, aren't you a cute one. My daughter would love you. Too bad you're a Pit Bull. My wife would have a fit if I came home with *you*."

I sat back down again and cocked my head at the man. I whimpered a plea. "Take me. Take me, please. I promise you I'll be a Good Dog."

He shook his head. "No, don't try to convince me. You aren't the one. Cute as you are, I can't take you home with me."

I sighed and hung my head as he walked away.

And then I heard a voice—a young, female voice. "Oh, my," she said, coming up to my Cage. "Is this the Pit Bull pup you were telling me about?"

The Shelter Worker was close on her heels. "Yes, that's the one. He needs a home right away. He's been here too long already. Sweetest pup you'll ever meet."

The woman—girl—I'm not sure what she was, sank down on the floor, so she was at eye level with me. "But he's beautiful. Look at those white markings on his chest—and that white stripe down his face. And his rich brown color. Look at those sweet, sweet eyes. He's a lovely puppy and bound to be a handsome dog."

She put her hand on the mesh of my Cage. I hurried up and licked her fingers. I looked deep into *her* eyes. *Take me*, I said, putting all I had into it. *Please take me home with you. This is my last chance.*

"I don't know," she said, the doubt and indecision in her voice wounding my heart. "I didn't come here for a puppy—and certainly not for a Pit Bull. What I really want is an older dog—already housebroken, past the chewing stage. You know, one I can leave home alone when I have to go to class. I have such a full schedule. I'm studying to be a veterinarian, and it's grueling actually."

"Then I'm sure you would be a *great* owner for him. Pit Bulls are not for everyone. Not everyone understands them or will give them the time they need. But you could fit it all in somehow—and anyway, if you don't take him…. Well, I'm afraid that today is his last day."

The girl turned to look at the Shelter Worker. The corners of her mouth dipped downward in what I now knew for certain was a frown of deep disapproval. "What do you mean—*his last day?*"

"I mean—we need his Cage for a more adoptable dog. I've been told to…to take him Down The Hall. You know, to the room where we…we put unwanted animals to sleep.

"Oh!" the girl exclaimed. "You're getting rid of him *today?*"

The Shelter Worker nodded. "I shouldn't say anything—but it's such a shame. No one wants a Pit Bull. He's the sweetest thing. But no one wants him."

"Well, *I* want him," the girl said, jumping to her feet. "I'll take him. I don't know how I'll make it work but I will. This puppy has a new home. I'll take him with me right now."

And that is how I got adopted by a girl—a young woman—whose name was Allison, I soon learned. Except everyone calls her Ally… like the place where I was born.

We must have been meant for each other—Ally and I.

As Ally was fitting a new collar around my neck, she said: "I'm going to call him Jack. This is my new dog, Jack, and I just know we are going to be the Best of Friends."

CHAPTER FOUR

The Best Of Friends

Ally lived in a teeny, tiny apartment near the campus of the university where she was studying to be a veterinarian.

Not that I understood any of that on the day she took me home with her. I was so happy to be leaving the shelter that I danced all around her as she led me up the front walk of her apartment building. It was a big old building that smelled of cooking food and musty old things. And People. Lots of People.

Ally lived on the third floor.

We had to take the steps. Since I was still too small to climb steps—had never even seen them before—Ally carried me up the steps all the way to her apartment. We went inside and Ally took off my leash and immediately began spreading papers—newspapers, they were called—all over the bare wooden floor that was all scuffed and scratched. It did have one covering—a square thing with faded color right in the middle of the room, the rug, I soon learned it was called.

"I shouldn't have done this, Jack," Ally said as she rustled newspapers. "I need a Pit Bull puppy like I need to fail one of my classes. I started out just wanting to get a dog—a guard-type dog. Or at least a mean-looking dog. Even though the university is here, it's kind of a rough neighborhood. Having a dog would be good.... Besides, I've so missed having animals around. I've never *not* had animals in my life—sharing my life—until I came here to University."

Ally sat down on the floor in the middle of the faded rug and took me into her lap. She turned me on my back and started to scratch my tummy. I wanted to explore, so I wiggled and tried to get free.

But, then I remembered: I was going to be a Good Dog. The best dog ever. I never wanted Ally to be sorry she had taken me home with her and saved me from having to go Down The Hall. So I made myself lie still and let her do whatever she wanted. It was very pleasant listening to Ally talk to me while she scratched itches I didn't know I had.

"I grew up on a farm, Jack. It's nothing like here in the city. We had dogs, cats, cows, ducks, chickens—you name it. I grew up around animals and I love them. All I ever wanted to be was a vet, so I could take care of animals. Now, here I am—in the Big City working hard to make that dream come true."

She lifted me up and looked me in the eye. "But this is a very Big City, Jack. Nothing like where I come from. And it's lonely. All I do is study, go to class—and work in the Second-Time-Around Shop to help pay for every-thing. I've no time for a social life…. Well, *you* are going to be my social life. I can come home between classes and see you, take you out, play with you…. With you around, I won't feel lonely at all."

She smiled at me, then put her lips right on my nose and…and *kissed* me. I didn't know it was a kiss, at the time—but I knew it gave me good feelings. It made me so happy. This was My Human. My Very Own Human—and she wanted me. *Needed* me. I could see it in her eyes.

She rubbed her face against the side of *my* face. "We're going to have wonderful times together, Jack. I know it. You'll be here waiting for me when I get home. And we can go to the park, take a run down by the river, have picnics together…. I'll teach you everything you need to know to be a City dog. A *Good* Dog. I used to take my old dog, Pogo, to obedience class—and later to agility classes. He was my best friend until he passed away at a ripe old age. I've been wanting a new dog ever since, and *you*, Jack, are *it*."

Ally set me down on the floor then. "Go ahead and look around," she said. "I've got to set up a crate for you, so you have a safe place to stay whenever I'm gone."

A crate? Did that mean a *Cage?*

Suddenly, I was not too happy about *that* idea.

"Oh, don't worry," Ally said, grinning and shaking her head at me as if she knew what I was thinking. "You'll learn to like it. It won't be at all like your Cage in the shelter. Once you're housebroken, you'll be able to come and go as you please. I'll only shut you up in it when I absolutely have to. It will become like your den—a place to rest and call your own. A place with a comfy bed in it and maybe a few chew toys."

I was still doubtful but I put my paws up on her knee and wagged my tail. "I promise you, Jack," she said, scratching behind my ears. "You are going to *Love* our life together. I'll do all I can to keep you healthy and happy. We're a team now, you and me. Neither of us is alone any more. From now on, we have each other. Forever and always."

Forever and Always. I *Loved* the sound of that.

I gazed up into her beautiful face—and right into her big blue eyes. She had light-colored hair, almost yellow, with a little brown in it, I noticed. And she had a sprinkling of little brown dots across her nose and two little dents, one at each corner of her mouth, as if someone had pushed in the spots with a finger. She had a wide, kind mouth. A mouth made for smiling. In her eyes, I saw warmth and laughter. I saw kindness. I saw the beginnings of True and Lasting Love.

And I *felt* Love.

Yes, I *Loved* Ally—suddenly, instantly, with my whole heart. I Loved her with a Love That Would Last Forever. Until I drew my last breath on this earth and returned to The Place I Had Come From, I would Love my Ally.

My Love for her would be My Purpose. I would be her Best Friend. I would make her laugh when she was Sad or Lonely. I would remind her when it was time to go for walks, eat her meals, or play. I would protect her when she slept and listen attentively to all her problems. I would do anything she asked, learn anything she wanted to teach me. I would try, anyway. Try as hard as I could to be a Good Dog.

"Arf!" I said, trying to let her know that I agreed with everything she had told me.

"Let me show you around then. My apartment is small but it has everything I need. Or at least it does now that *you're* here."

That first night with Ally was wonderful. She did not even seem to mind that I could not help myself and did My Business where I should not have—*off* the newspapers she had put down for me. During the night, when I awoke and got scared and worried being in a strange place, she took me up into bed with her and cuddled me close until I fell asleep again. And in the morning, when we awoke, she rushed me outside where I did My Business on the grass—the new green grass.

I had never seen grass before. Only concrete. And I loved it. The air was still chilly but new green things seemed to be popping up everywhere.

"It's spring, Jack," Ally said. "Can you smell it?

Yes, I could. It smelled wonderful—all fresh and new and green and growing.

So this is what the world is like away from alleys, Cages and Animal Shelters, I thought to myself as I ran around sniffing.

It was a *wonderful* place.

So began a pattern for our days and nights.

During the day, Ally had to go to class while I had to stay in my crate, lined with newspapers, in case I had an "accident."

The last thing I wanted to do was to have an Accident. So I slept while I waited for Ally to come back home again. When she did, she would take me straight away down the stairs and outside onto the green grass. And in this way, I learned not to have Accidents.

No dog likes to lie in his own waste and will do anything he can to avoid it. I learned to keep myself from doing My Business until Ally came home and took me down to the grass. Her apartment was close to her school, so she was able to come home often and take care of me.

At first, I was so lonely whenever she left that I wanted to bark and whine and scrabble at the door to my crate. I would start whining even before she left. But Ally would gently correct me and remind me to be quiet. And when she came home from wherever she had gone, if I stayed quiet until she opened the gate of my crate, she would give me a Special Treat. A yummy, chewy little bite of something that came out of a bag and smelled so good it made me drool and slobber on myself.

I learned to do many things that she patiently taught me, one delicious treat at a time. I learned to sit on command, come when she called my name, and lay down and stay when she said Stay. Staying was the hardest thing I had to do. I never wanted to leave Ally's side when she was home—and I certainly did not want to Sit and Stay or even worse, do a Down Stay.

I had too much energy. The Best Thing was when she went and got the leash and I knew I was going outside to do My Business and maybe Go For A Walk. In no time at all, my ability to speak Human became second nature. I knew from the tone of Ally's voice what she wanted, even if the words did not make much sense. Eventually, I mastered the words, too.

Sit. Stay. Down. Heel. Come. Ally drilled me in the commands until I could have done them in my sleep. Sometimes I did do them in my sleep. I dreamed of them—and I dreamed of Ally smiling so happily at me when I did as she asked.

She always praised me and told me what a Good Dog I was. And she gave me those wonderful treats for obeying. I wanted so much to please her and see her eyes light up. "What a Smart Dog you are!" she would say. "You are still just a pup, but you understand everything, don't you? You learn the fastest of any dog I've ever seen."

Of course, I thought, bursting with pride. I am a Pit Bull. And Pit Bulls are Smart.

By this time, I could even read Ally's thoughts—most of the time, anyway. I knew when she was happy, sad or worried. If she was sad or worried, I considered it my job to make her Happy—to make her smile again. Which she did quite often, I am pleased to say, because I was so good at my job.

When we went for walks, People would sometimes stop us to ask: "Is that a Pit Bull?"

"Yes," Ally would say with a very big grin. "This is Jack and he is a sweet obedient dog. Sit, Jack."

And I would sit. Smiling at a potential new friend.

"Shake, Jack." And Ally would hold out her hand while I lifted my paw so she could take it and shake it. Shaking was another one of the commands I had mastered.

"My, that's certainly a well-behaved dog—and a Pit Bull, too. Who would have thought?"

Sometimes I got a pat on my head from these strangers. And afterward, when we walked on, with me following at Ally's side in the Heel position, Ally would laugh and say: "You know what you are, Jack? You are an Ambassador For Your Breed."

Whatever *that* was.

I only knew that when Ally was Happy, I was Happy. We had a Good Life. And I grew and grew, turning into a full grown dog, all muscle, strength and smartness, trotting along beside my Human and thinking I was Hot Stuff.

Through warm season or cold, Ally and I enjoyed our lives together. We played on the grass at the park, where I chased Frisbees, we played in the snow where I tried to catch snowballs, we spent long evenings together studying, Ally with her nose in a book and me with my nose between my paws on the floor at her feet.

If the weather turned bad and we had to stay inside, even then we always found something fun to do—Tug of War, Chase the Tennis Ball, and my favorite game of all—Catch The Bubbles. Ally kept a blue bottle of something liquid up on the top shelf of her closet, and whenever she went there to fetch it, I always knew what was coming: "Jack, do you want to play Catch the Bubbles?"

Of course, I did! I would wiggle and squirm and whimper—but not bark, because I wasn't supposed to bark inside the apartment—while she got down the blue bottle. She would carefully remove a stick-like thing inside it and wave it in the air, or blow on it. And wonderful shiny, round things would suddenly float through the air for me to catch. I would snap at them and chase them and jump up high to get them, but they always popped in my face and my jaws closed around nothing but air.

Ally would laugh and laugh. Usually we wound up wrestling on the rug at the end, and then Ally would sigh contentedly and say something like: "Oh, you are such a Good Dog, Jack. Such a wonderful antidote for bad weather, or a bad test grade, or too little money, or too much to do and not enough time to do it in."

She would scratch behind my ears and snuggle with me. No matter what happens, you are always there for me—and I'll always be there for *you*, Jack."

And she was.

If Ally had a Hamburger, a Hot Dog or a piece of toast, she saved the last bite for me. Only sometimes would she say, "No, Jack. This wouldn't be such a great snack for a dog. So none of this for you, buddy."

She always had my best interests at heart—and I always had *her* best interests at heart. I think that's what Love is, when all is said and done. You know you can trust Someone to look out for you and your best interests, no matter what. If you make a mistake, you will be forgiven. If your feelings get hurt by something thoughtlessly said or done to you, *your* forgiveness will be sought. Your special Someone will try to make it right. When Bad Things happen—as they sometimes do—you won't face them alone. And you won't let your Loved One face things alone, either.

Yes, that's what Love is, all right. And that's what Ally and I had.

We were inseparable—Ally and her Pit Bull, Jack. Sometimes, she even took me to school with her, where I became quite popular, along with Ally, among her student friends. Because of me, People wanted to get to know Ally.

Before me, before I came into her life, Ally admitted in one of our heart-to-heart talks, she did not have that many friends at school. She was just another hard-working student among hundreds of other students struggling to master difficult subjects.

But after I became a part of Ally's life, she soon had many friends. I was a Conversation Starter, as she called it. At the very least, People wanted to know if I was Dangerous.

"About as dangerous as a cupcake," Ally would say, laughing. "And twice as sweet."

Sometimes, People came by our apartment. They would eat and drink and play music—and drop food on the floor, which I always cleaned up immediately. I loved those times—until the time that a new friend came to see Ally. He was someone she had just met. Someone from school, I assumed.

He came with a bunch of her friends that I had already met at previous parties Ally had held in our apartment. Ally and her friends ordered pizza and I became very excited when I smelled it, as the pizza delivery man came up the stairs and knocked on our door.

Pizza is delicious. And I knew there would be crusts. Someone would be sure to drop a crust or a piece of pepperoni on the floor for me to find, especially as the party heated up. Ally put the pizza on the round table where she always put food when she ate. But she didn't take a piece or start to eat it. She was drinking from a green bottle. Her New Friend—a tall young man with a lot of black hair—kept urging her to drink more and more.

He took out a flat silver bottle from inside his jacket, grabbed a glass from the cupboard, poured some brown liquid into the glass, and held it out to Ally.

"Here, have some," he said. "It's great stuff—will make this party really lively."

I could smell the liquid from where I was sitting underneath the table; it had a sharp tang to it—a tang that would make my eyes water if I got close enough to stick my nose in it.

"What is it?" Ally asked. She was flushed from having finished off the contents of at least two of the green bottles.

"Just a little whiskey. Jack Daniels."

Jack? The brown liquid in the glass had the same name as *me?*

"I really shouldn't," Ally said, waving the glass away. "I've already drunk too much beer. I'm not much for holding my liquor."

"Oh, come on," her new friend said. "It won't hurt you. Besides, shouldn't we be celebrating? We're on the home stretch now, honey. Not long 'til graduation. Just one more semester and we're outa here—only a few short months. Gotta celebrate starting our last semester."

"Oh, all right. Since you insist, Todd." Ally reached for the glass. She took it, put it to her lips, and drank it down fast. Then she gasped and hiccupped, laughing and putting a hand to her mouth. "Oh, my g—gosh!" she sputtered. Tears streamed down her cheeks.

Todd—that was her new friend's name—grabbed her hand and pulled her to her feet. "Come on," he said. "Let's dance, pretty lady. I wanna hold you close."

I watched all this from underneath the table. Something about this Todd was all wrong. I didn't like him grabbing my Ally and pulling her close to him. Didn't like the way he held her so tight. Didn't like the feel of his energy. Ally's energy was always light, bright, and warm—like sunshine. But this Todd was dark, nothing at all like Ally. He was like the dark and cold. Like Winter. Or maybe a Thunderstorm.

It grew later and later. Ally's friends began to say their goodbyes and leave. I needed to go downstairs and do My Business. I wanted Todd to say goodbye and leave so Ally and I could clean up the mess they had made of her apartment. There were pizza crusts and green bottles everywhere. I no longer even wanted the pizza crusts. I just wanted the night to end and to have Ally to myself again.

Soon, everyone had grabbed their coats and jackets off Ally's bed, put them on and left. Everyone but Todd, that is. He took out his flat silver bottle and poured more whiskey for Ally. "Come on, baby. Drink up," he urged. "The party's just beginning."

"Ish late, Todd, You need t' go home. I need t' take Jack down t' go potty—shnotty." Ally giggled, sounding all funny and different. "I can't even talk shtraight. What a night."

"Come on, baby. Drink a little more. You'll be fine. All you stand to lose are your inhibitions…. " Todd held the glass of brown liquid to Ally's lips. "Not bad things to lose, Ally, baby. Not bad at all. Been waiting all night for you to lose your damn inhibitions…and to get you alone."

I growled. I couldn't help myself. It was just a low growl—a warning. I wanted to let Ally know that I didn't trust this guy. Didn't trust him one bit—and she shouldn't, either.

But Ally drank more of the liquid in the glass—and after that, things got Ugly.

Todd grabbed Ally around the waist and steered her backwards toward the bedroom and her bed. Ally could hardly walk. She leaned into Todd and let him do what he wanted. Halfway to the bedroom, Ally sagged in Todd's arms and slipped right down to the floor. Her eyes were half-closed, and she seemed to have no strength in her arms and legs. Her legs could not hold her up anymore.

"Not here, baby," Todd said. "At least, let me get you to the bed. Oh, yes, let me get you into bed finally."

He half-dragged, half-carried Ally to her bed and laid her out flat on it. Only one last jacket still lay on the edge of the bed and he shoved it aside so that it fell on the floor. Its scent reached my nose and I realized that it must he *his* jacket because it held his particular scent, which I was beginning to hate. I wrinkled my nose in disgust and pushed closer to the bed, determined to protect Ally if she needed protecting.

"Ally?" Todd slapped her lightly on the cheek. "Ally, baby?"

When she just moaned and turned her head away, he bent over her and started popping buttons off her blouse. He began pawing at her and tearing at her clothes.

This was too much. I sprang into action. He was going to hurt my Ally. I *knew* it. I could smell his excitement and his evil intent. He *wanted* to hurt my Ally.

I flew around the side of the bed and grabbed at his pant leg, growling and pulling, trying to drag him away from Ally as she lay still and unmoving, not seeing or hearing me. Not seeing or hearing this *Todd* guy, either. I pulled as hard as I could, trying to get him away from her.

"What the hell...?" Todd turned and kicked at me. His foot connected with my ribs and sent me flying across the room.

"Get away from me, you damn dog!" he hollered.

I knew what I had to do. I had to stop him from doing Something Bad to Ally.

And that was how I turned into a vicious Pit Bull fighting to save my Best Friend.

CHAPTER FIVE

The Vicious Pit Bull

The trouble was, I had never bitten anyone. I did not know how. And it went against everything Ally had ever taught me and everything I believed about myself. I had long ago made up my mind *never* to hurt anyone. Never to be a Bad Dog like that. Ally would be shocked to think that I even *wanted* to bite someone. Biting someone would be worse than…than peeing on the bed or tearing up her pillow.

So I snapped at Todd and growled and barked. I raced at his legs and tore at his pants. But I did not do that one Bad Thing that I knew I should not do—the thing that would Disappoint Ally and get me into Big Trouble.

I did not sink my teeth into Todd's leg. Though I thought about it, and I sure *wanted* to bite him.

And Todd thought I was going to. "Don't you bite me!" he cried, edging back toward the door. "Damn dog. What's she doing with a Pit Bull, anyway? It oughta be against the law to have a vicious dog like you!"

I put myself between Ally and Todd, the fur on my back standing on end. I bared my teeth and told Todd in no uncertain terms that if he came a step nearer, if he tried to hurt my Ally, I *would* bite him. And once I bit, I would not let go. I would bite straight through to the bone and hold on forever.

"Okay," he said. "*Okay.* You win. I'm leaving."

Grabbing one of the empty green bottles off the table as he left the bedroom, he hurled it at me, turned and ran—rushing toward the door to the apartment. When he left, he left the door to the apartment standing wide open.

The bottle missed me and bounced off the leg of the bed.

Once I was sure he was gone, his footsteps fading in the stairwell, I went to Ally and nosed her hand.

She didn't move. Worried, I jumped up on the bed and listened to her breathing. It did not sound right. It was somehow different than usual. I knew how she normally sounded when she slept. I had slept in her bed with her often enough. She usually invited me up sometime during the night and I would curl up beside her—the two of us breathing in unison. Breathing deep and slow. I could time my own breaths to Ally's and breathe as if the two of us were only one Person—or one Dog.

Those times were nothing at all like she was breathing now. Her breathing definitely did not sound right. She would breathe in and her breath would catch. Actually stop for a moment. Then she would shudder slightly before breathing out. There were long pauses between each breath, as if another breath might not be coming.

I was scared—as scared as I had ever been. I didn't know what to do. I was more scared for Ally than I had ever been for myself, even when I thought they were going to take me Down The Hall at the Animal Shelter.

I nosed her face and neck. I licked her cheek. She did not awaken. She smelled different, too. It was not her usual warm sweet Ally smell.

I jumped off the bed and turned in a fast circle on the floor a moment, trying to decide what to do. Maybe I could wake her if I barked. Barked really loud. If the bark did *not* wake her, it would at least tell someone else in the building that something was very wrong with my Ally.

There was the nice lady one floor down who liked to pat me and scratch behind my ears. She always smelled funny and liked to wear stuff on top of her head—a scarf or a hat, I had learned they were called.

There was the man on the first floor who cleaned the building and changed the light bulbs in the stairwell. Maybe if I barked my loudest, he would come up the stairs to see what was wrong.

So I stood at the foot of the bed and began to bark. I barked and barked.

Ally never stirred. Never lifted her head to see what was the matter or to tell me to hush. I barked my heart out.

Yes. Someone was coming—the Man Who Changed Light Bulbs.

"What in tarnation is wrong up here!" he shouted, sounding angry as he tromped up the stairs. "Ally? Ally, where are you?... Jack, why in thunder are you barking this time of night? Never seen you make such a dang racket before."

He came through the open doorway of the apartment, and I ran back and forth between the front room and the bedroom—showing him the way and barking all the time. He had his baggy pants on, which I had seen before, but his shirt was not tucked in and he was wearing flapping slippers, not shoes. I had not seen those before either, but Ally had slippers, so I knew what slippers were.

"Good Lord," he grunted, seeing Ally sprawled on the bed.

He went over to her, saw how she was lying so still and breathing so funny and he went into action. He pulled out his cell phone—Ally had one, too, so I knew what it was—and began punching it with one finger.

"Hello? Hello?" he hollered into it. "I need an ambulance right away."

He said some more things but I was too worried about Ally to listen. I jumped up on the bed again and lay down next to her as close as I could get. I had this fear—this Terrible Fear. I was afraid that Ally might be Going Back To Where She Came From.

I could smell it on her. She was getting ready to leave. I was sending her thoughts but something was blocking them. I was calling her back, begging her not to leave, but she didn't seem to know I was there. All I could do was whimper and nose her still fingers. She didn't hear me—didn't hear me at all. Not my thoughts, my whines, nor my whimpers. She was somewhere far away—and might be going further still. And soon.

No, Ally. No.

I shivered and shook. I just kept trying to talk to her, to reach her, to beg her to stay.

A short time later, I heard the shrill shriek of a siren—and moments after that, the bedroom filled up with Humans who had come to help Ally.

I tried to stay out of their way. I knew they were Good People. Not like Todd. Dogs can tell about things like that when it comes to protecting their owners. Just as I could read Todd's energy, I could read the energy of those who came to help my Ally.

Ally's rescuers lifted Ally onto a flat thing so they could carry her down the steps. They were going to take her away somewhere. I jumped around to remind them that they needed to take me, too. No way was I leaving my Ally. Nor was she leaving me. Wherever she went I was going, too. It was my job to stay right by her side and protect her.

But as they were carrying Ally out the door on the "stretcher" as one of the Humans called it, one of the rescuers, a female, turned and said: "What about her dog? Can you look after him?"

She said this to the Man Who Changed Light Bulbs. "Sure. Guess I can," he grumbled. "For a few days, anyway. Do you think she'll be all right? Will she be home again soon?"

"Hard to tell at this point. Her vitals aren't good. You probably saved her life, calling us when you did. Have you ever known her to take drugs of any kind?"

"Drugs? Ally? No…no. She's gonna be a vet'rinarian. Gonna graduate end of this school year. She's straight as they come. Lived here all the time she's been at the university. Never been a lick of trouble—except maybe a party now and then like t'night. Her parties can get a little noisy sometimes, but they're not too bad."

"Well, she's gotten into serious trouble this time. Just take care of her dog for her. If by some chance, you *can't* look after him—or she doesn't make it back, after all—you'll have to take the dog to an Animal Shelter."

"My God. That bad, is it?"

"Well, it's either alcohol poisoning—or drugs. Neither scenario is looking good. If you know how to get in touch with her family, please do so immediately."

No. *No.*

I was going with Ally. I had to be with my Ally. I rushed down the stairwell ahead of the rescuers who were already maneuvering Ally down the turns of the stairwell.

"Come back here, Jack!" called the Man Who Changed Light Bulbs. "Dang it, you come back here right now."

But I had spotted the long red and white vehicle waiting for my Ally. They were going to load her into it on her stretcher once they came down the stairs. The back door to it stood wide open, so I jumped inside. Surely, now that I was in here, they would let me stay with her.

But it was not to be. They grabbed my collar and pulled me out of the ambulance, shoved Ally's stretcher inside and slammed the door in my face. With red lights flashing and siren screaming, hurting my ears—hurting my heart, the ambulance pulled away from me and started to go faster and faster.

The only thing I could do was follow. I raced after the ambulance, running as fast as I could to keep up. I couldn't let it get away from me. I couldn't...*couldn't*...

"Jack! Jack! Come back here!" hollered The Man Who Changed Light Bulbs.

I could *not* go back. I had to stay with Ally. Had to follow the ambulance.

The tags on my collar jangled as I chased it as fast as I could possibly run.

CHAPTER SIX

Alone and Lost

I could not keep up.

Could not even see where the ambulance went.

Still, I ran on—hoping to catch a glimpse of it.

It was no use.

I stopped in the middle of the street and stared hard in the direction where the ambulance had gone. I kept hoping I would see it. I was panting and out of breath. A puff of white rose from my mouth and nose to float around my head in the cold night air. My heart was pounding.

A car came barreling around the corner and almost ran me down. I jumped sideways in the nick of time to keep from getting run over—but when I jumped sideways, I landed in front of another car.

Cars were suddenly coming at me out of nowhere. Horns blared at me. One guy leaned out of his window and hollered: "Get out of the street, you stupid dog!"

I realized I needed to move—but which way? What direction? Should I find my way home and wait for Ally there? Should I keep trying to track down the long red and white ambulance?

While I debated these issues, cars whizzed past me. One came so close that it almost touched my nose. I jumped backwards—and that was when it happened.

Whomp! I went flying through the air. The asphalt rushed up to meet me. And I landed with such a hard whack that it knocked the breath from me. Little shards of light exploded in my head. Then I could see nothing. Hear nothing. Everything had stopped.

That was all I remembered—until a man nudged me with his foot.

"Hey, Dawg," he muttered. "You still alive? Or have you gone to meet your Maker?"

Slowly, I came awake to find myself sprawled on the curb with cars still rushing past me—only a short distance from my head.

Oh, but I hurt so bad. I hurt all over. My head hurt the worst. I didn't know if I could move. I couldn't feel my legs. I could hardly breathe. I was shivering from the cold and from my own reactions to what had happened to me.

"Dawg, you too close to the street. You gonna get hit again. You gotta re-locate. Come on, now."

The man reached down and grabbed hold of my collar and—seemingly unaware of how much pain he was causing me—dragged me across the pavement away from the traffic. And he didn't stop there. He dragged me a bit further into a long narrow space that some part of me recognized as an alley.

An alley.

It smelled a lot like the place where I was born. It had that distinctive alley odor. This one was full of trashcans and boxes and junk piled everywhere. And it was dark—with only a single bare light bulb burning over a doorway down at the far end of the long, narrow space.

"Come on, Dawg. Get up. Can't you walk? You hurt, boy? You hurt bad?"

I hurt too bad to even make a sound. Too bad to move. All I could do was lie there and let the man drag me into the alley, to a space behind a pile of boxes.

"Okay, Dawg. We're here now. You can rest now, boy. Gotta rest me a spell, too."

The man sank down beside me—sat on the ground on top of a pile of smelly blankets next to some trash bags. Leaning back against the building, he sighed and closed his eyes—all the while keeping one hand tucked inside my collar as if I might get away. But I wasn't going anywhere. If I fell asleep—and I thought I might—I didn't know if I would wake up again.

"Whew. You done wore me out, boy. Draggin' you outa harm's way. Let's just set here and rest a spell before we th nk on what to do next."

That was fine by me. As I said, I wasn't going anywhere. I could not even think where I was—or how I had gotten there. It was as if everything—all my thoughts, memories, worries and fears—had been knocked clean out of me. I hardly knew *who* I was, much less *where* I was.

So I just lay there and let the darkness creep over me again.

When next I woke, it was getting light. I opened my eyes and realized that it was morning. I lay there for a while trying to remember. What was I doing here? How had I gotten here? Something warm and cozy-feeling had been wrapped around me while I slept—though I still felt chilled and shivery.

I turned my head and saw the man, leaning back against the building with his eyes closed and his mouth open. He was snoring—and coughing a little at the end of each snore. I could smell him.

He smelled of…of Jack Daniels. The thought just popped into my head. I had smelled that smell before, or something similar, and knew I did not like it. But I could not remember *why*.

The man seemed nice enough. He was certainly harmless. But oh, he stunk. Stunk of Jack Daniels or something like it, and old, dirty clothes, and body odor as strong or stronger than I have ever smelled on a Human. A gray stubble covered his face and stringy brownish gray hair hung down from beneath a battered old hat. He wore old clothes that were torn and dirty—a long coat over several other layers of clothing. I knew it was still the dark and cold time, but the time of year that I loved would be coming eventually. It always did follow the cold time—soon enough, it would be spring again. When things were new, green and growing. When new grass came up lush and earthy-smelling…

It had been springtime when…when…

Something very important had happened in my life during the springtime. But I could no. all what it was exactly. I rolled onto my belly, dislodging the blanket that had covered me, and whimpered in surprise. I hurt everywhere—from nose to tail. Everything around me was suddenly spinning—going faster whenever I moved my head. I sighed and lowered my head onto my paws.

I was thirsty. I wanted my bowl of water. That much I remembered. I had a water bowl somewhere and it was kept full of clean water for me to drink whenever I wanted it.

I had a food bowl, too. Every single day it was filled morning and night with Kibble, topped with something meaty, moist and delicious. But who filled it? Who took care of me? Where did I live? Where was Home?

I knew I had a Home somewhere. A Home with a water bowl and a food bowl and…and…someone who…who…

I could not remember. I only knew that Something Huge was missing. Once I had had it, and now, I did not. I was all alone now. Well, not quite alone because there was the snoring man next to me. But he wasn't someone I knew. He wasn't someone important to me. He was a stranger actually. He had nothing to do with me or my life. He wasn't who I wanted.

I need to go Home, I thought, and I tried to get up.

Ouch! My back leg did not want to work. I managed to push myself upright with my other three legs, but the fourth leg—that back one—would not hold me. And it hurt. It hurt so bad whenever I tried to move it. I could not even think of putting it down and making it take my weight and do its share of helping me walk. I stood there, trembling, trying hard to stay balanced on three shaky legs.

This was a heck of a fix. How was I going to go Home if I couldn't walk on all four legs?

The man must have heard me, because he coughed, lifted a hand to his eyes and rubbed his face. Then he opened his eyes and looked at me. His eyes were pale and had little lines radiating out from them. He blinked as if he could hardly see out of them.

"Well, lookit you, Dawg. You goin' somewheres?"

I was shaking so hard from pain and the exertion of standing on three legs, carefully keeping the fourth one off the ground, that I thought I had better lie down again before I fell down. I was clearly in danger of falling.

"Not feelin' too good, huh?" the man said. "No wonder. You dang near got yourself run over last night, Dawg. Don't know what you thought you was doin', standin' out there in the middle of the street with cars whizzin' past."

I licked a front paw, then turned my head around and tried to lick my sore back leg. It was throbbing so bad. All I knew to do was lick it. But even as I worried it—licking and chewing it, trying to remove the pain—I knew it wasn't going to get better anytime soon. I might be three-legged for the rest of my life. The agony of my situation made me tremble and jerk a little with each lick.

"You'll be okay, Dawg." The man reached over, quite unexpectedly, and patted my head. "Name's Ned," he said. "Ned Wharton. Or used to be Wharton, anyway. Don't use my last name much anymore. Got no need for it. What's your name, hey?"

I ignored him and kept right on licking.

"All right. Be that way. I'll call you Dawg, then. Better we don't get too friendly, anyhow. I sure as hell can't keep no dawg—not with the life I lead. I'm a travelin' man, y' see. I go where the wind takes me. Never know fer sure where I am or where I'm goin' next. Do an odd job here and there, if I can get it. Go to a shelter and get a free meal when I can't and my monthly dole done run out. But mostly I jus' live on the street, Dawg. It's a hell of a life."

His hand slid down and lingered on my collar. He fingered my tags—my shiny silver tags. "Seems t' me you is a fancy Dawg, anyway. Used t' the Good Life. You're a handsome fellah leastways. All shiny fur. No ribs showin'. Eyes all bright, except fer the hurtin' look in 'em. Yep. You've had a fine life. Wonder how you wound up out there in the middle of the street. Wonder if your owner is lookin' fer ya. Might be your owner wants ya back again and would be willin' t' pay to get you."

I stopped licking and looked at him. My owner. M-Y O-W-N-E-R.

My Ally…. *Where was my Ally?*

Memories came back in a rush. I had to go. Three legged or not, hurt or not, I had to find Ally. I pushed myself back up again, yelping when my sore leg touched the ground and I yanked it up again. I would just have to run on three legs. I could do it. I had to do it. *I had to find Ally.*

"Hey! Where you think you're goin', Dawg?" The man grabbed my collar and hung on. "You can't go runnin' off on three legs. You'll just get hit by a car, again. Or they'll pick you up and cart you down to the Animal Shelter and lock you up. Throw away the key. You'll never come out again most likely."

The Animal Shelter.

Ally would not know to look for me there. Besides, my Ally was hurt! They had taken *her* away to get help for her. And if I got caught and taken to the Animal Shelter, hurt as I was, they would march me Down The Hall right away. That's what they did with hurt dogs no one wanted, the ones

46

who weren't "adoptable." Suddenly, I could recall every miserable detail of a dog's life—*my* former life—in the Animal Shelter before Ally had rescued me and made me her dog. Her Good Dog.

I stood there trembling—consumed with the need to go look for Ally but unsure of what to do or where to go. I had no idea where they had taken her. The city was a big place. She could be anywhere. I was not even sure where Home was. I would have to work hard to find it. And if I found it, would she even be there? I didn't think so. They had taken her away, after all.

And I had no strength. No strength at all.

Just standing on three legs—hurting all over—so stiff and sore I could scarcely move, made me feel so weak that I feared I might fall down at any minute.

What could I do? What *should* I do? I had no idea.

"Now, listen here, Dawg. How about you and me hang out together for a bit? Just while your leg is gettin' better. Then, when it's all better, we'll see about takin' you back home again. It says something right here on your tag—probably it's your address where you live. Let me see—hang on now—"

The man squinted his eyes and leaned closer. "Yep, it's your address. But I ain't never heard of that street. And wait a minute…it's got your name here, too. Jack," he said. "It says your name is Jack."

At the sound of my name—spoken by a stinky stranger—I let out a sharp bark.

"Well, then, Dawg. I guess your name is Jack. Except you look more like a Dawg to me. I think I'll just call you Dawg, after all. Your life as Jack is over, anyway. Hell if I know that street where you live. We might never be able to find that street. Too bad 'cause I could use the reward money if any was offered."

I heard what he was saying. And I wanted to insist that he call me by my name—the name Ally had given me. "My name is Jack!" I barked. "Do you get it? Jack. And I belong to Ally. She's my Best Friend. I'm her Good Dog."

But Ned seemed not to understand. Humans usually *don't* understand dogs. We can speak Human, but that doesn't mean Humans can speak Dog. Only a few—a precious few like my Ally—can speak Dog.

Or even make the effort to try.

"Hush, now, hush...." Ned said, unbuckling my collar, removing the tags from it, sticking them in his pocket, and then re-buckling the collar around my neck.

"You got a new owner now, Dawg. No need for barkin' or whinin'. Guess I better think about getting you some water and somethin' t' eat. It's not easy livin' out on the street. But I manage. Yep, I do. And you'll manage, too.... Lots of times, there's stuff t' eat in trash bins. Did you know that? I know some really good ones—ones outside restaurants, the best restaurants in town. If a body's careful not to get caught, you can always eat. I'll show you the ropes, Dawg. You stick with old Ned, and he'll show you the ropes. Had me an old coon hound once. Know all about dawgs. Yep, I do. And you an' me, we is buddies, now. Right? We is buddies."

And that was how I became a Street Dawg. Because really—at this point in my life—I had little choice.

CHAPTER SEVEN

Street Dawg

Ned was as good as his word.

He showed me "the ropes" of living rough on the street.

We ate from trashcans and dumpsters in alleys behind the city's best restaurants. Ned knew them all—and knew to wait until "the wee hours of the morning", as he called them, before carefully inspecting what had been thrown away.

Restaurants throw away a lot of food. And it's usually tasty—though some things Ned would not eat.

"That's nasty," he would say, when something smelled funny. "Can't eat that, Dawg. Not fit for man nor beast."

At times, especially when the weather was bad, we went to shelters where Ned went inside, leaving me outside chained to something in an alley. Ned had found a length of what he called a "chain"—very lightweight, but I could not chew through it as I could a piece of clothesline he once tried. The chain became a kind of leash. He never used it to keep me near him, because I stayed with him willingly without any restraint. He only used the chain to fasten or clip me to something when he had to leave me by myself, so that I would stay where he wanted me.

He didn't seem to realize that I already knew all my commands and probably would have stayed, anyway, if he had just said "Stay, Dawg."

When he came out again from a shelter—a Human Shelter, not an Animal Shelter—he always had food for me. Scraps, mostly, but once he brought me my own Hamburger tucked inside a big bun. I ate it, pickles and all, and thought I had never tasted anything better. It reminded me of that last bite of Hamburger my Ally had always shared with me. Ned could not believe I had eaten the pickles. He had pointed them out to me first, saying: "You like pickles, Dawg? If not, I'll eat 'em."

I ate them before he could even think about prying them off the melted cheese. Afterwards, I felt like a nap. I was very sad, remembering those days with Ally. I would never forget her. Never. But I also realized that wherever she was, she was gone. I could not just run off and find her, even if my leg was back to normal, which it wasn't. And might never be. My life had changed—and in the way of dogs everywhere, I accepted what I could not understand or make any different. I lived in the Present, letting each day unfold as it would.

We had a regular rou that—at this time of year—sometimes began and ended at a junkyard. In ain, wind or snow, which still occurred with some frequency, we could always find shelter huddled in blankets in the back seat of some rusty old abandoned car to wait out the worst of it. Once the weather began to clear, Ned would insist we leave. We always came and went through a tear in the fence around the junkyard. Ned didn't seem to want to meet up with anyone while we were there, and he didn't want anyone to spot us coming or going.

"Don't wanna get too comfy in some old junker," he would tell me, keeping his voice low. "They'll throw us out if they ever catch us—and they'll fix that fence so we can't get back inside again. Junkers is just for shelter when we absolutely need it, Dawg. We be fine on the street, anyway. Best place for folks like us."

Hopping along on three legs, I would try to keep up with Ned as he shuffled from street to street, alley to alley, carrying all his belongings in a black plastic trash bag. He did not own much—the smelly blankets and a few other things, which he seemed to treasure.

One thing in particular was his Favorite Thing. It was a picture frame with a likeness of someone in it. I did not know who the Person was, but Ned did.

"See this here, Dawg?" he would say whenever we had settled down for the night in an alley or under a bridge, if the night was clear, and he was sitting next to me pawing through his stuff, making sure it was all there.

"This here is my Bitsy—the gal I set my heart on. Called her Bitsy 'cause she was just a little bit of a thing. Pretty as a magnolia blossom and sweet, to boot. Had to leave her and go to war, I did. And while I was gone, she went and found somebody else. I come home all busted up from the war, and I had nobody. I was a wreck. Couldn't do nothin'. Couldn't find work even when I got better and my wounds healed. Couldn't hold a job when I found one. Had nightmares every night, and even some durin' the day."

He reached out to put a shaking hand on my head. "Bad thing, war is, Dawg. Ruins everything. Turns a man into someone he don't know anymore. Turns a man into a...a pitiful wreck. That's what I am—what I've become. A Pitiful Wreck far from home. Cain't even go back to where I come from down south of here. Could never hold my head up if'n I did. Could never let my Bitsy see what I've become. Not that she'd care much, Dawg, seein' as how she abandoned me, anyway."

I scooted closer to him and rested my head on his leg. I understood about Loving and Losing someone. And about turning into someone different from what you thought you were. It seemed I had lost my Ally. With my bum leg, I could not go looking for her. I could not walk very far without stopping and resting. The pain was almost constant and wore me down. It had turned me into a dog I hardly recognized. My old self would have been long gone hunting for Ally. My new self...well, was another dog entirely.

The truth was I needed Ned for food, water, warmth and shelter. He was not unkind to me. I think he needed me as much as I needed him. He wasn't my Ally but I was growing used to him—maybe even fond of him.

He kept me from feeling so dreadfully alone. And I think I did the same for him. Neither of us had the People we Loved anywhere nearby; so we might as well be together and do the best we could to make our way in the world.

"Yep, Dawg. Bitsy was the love of my life. I hope she's happy. She was the best. And even though I was mad as hell when she found someone else, that was for the best, too. Look at me…. I'm a bum now, livin' on a little dole money from the gov'mint, drinking it up mostly. And that's all I'll ever be—a bum. Nightmares ain't as bad as they used to be—but I still do get 'em sometimes. Still do get overcome by the Bad Times even when I'm awake."

I knew about Ned's nightmares—and about his Bad Times during the day, as well. I could always tell when he was having Bad Times. He would shiver, shake, groan and moan. He was afraid of People and stayed away from crowded places. He was most comfortable in dark, empty alleys or under bridges. Even then, he avoided other Humans who sometimes hid out in them, too.

I wouldn't say these were Bad Humans—it was more like they were Lost Humans. Bad Stuff had happened to them, and for some reason, they *wanted* to be alone like Ned and separate from other Humans. It was as if they didn't trust themselves to be with other Humans. Or didn't know how to behave around them.

Sometimes, when I felt the Bad Times coming on Ned, I would nose him—or even bark to get his attention. And he would start thinking about what I was trying to tell him instead of getting scared and thinking about Bad Stuff. Whatever the Bad Stuff was that had made him the way he was.

"Let's go find a dumpster," I would say, shoving my nose into his hand. "I'm hungry. Really, really *hungry.*"

And sometimes, he would actually get what I was saying and talk to me. "You wantin' some left over filly-mignon, Dawg? You got a powerful hankerin' for stuffed, baked potah-toes or spaghetti?"

"Yes, yes," I would say. "Let's go find some right now."

"Hmph. Dumpster Diver, that's what I've sunk to—me and my three-legged Dawg. We're Pitiful Wrecks and Dumpster Divers. That's what we are."

"Please, let's find a dumpster," I would shamelessly beg.

More often than not, my pleadings would work. We would head out from wherever we were and go in the direction of one of the restaurants we favored. When we got there, we often had to wait until The Right Time to go Dumpster Diving or searching through trashcans. A time when it was dark, everyone had left the restaurant of our choice, and no one was around to see us.

And sometimes, my pleadings would *not* work—I could not distract Ned no matter what I did. When that happened, Ned would find a way to buy a bottle of Jack Daniels or something that *smelled* like Jack Daniels. We would go to the Post Office to get what he called his mail, and then to the Bank, if he had gotten what he referred to as a Check, and then we would find a spot where he could sit and drink in peace, with me cuddled up beside him, guarding him while he worked on finishing off a whole bottle of whatever it was he was drinking that day.

I had once known about the Post Office—though it was different from the one Ally and I used to visit—and I knew about banks and checks, too. But with Ned, everything was different than it had been with Ally. And I mean *every*thing. Especially mealtimes.

When Ned was drinking, I got awfully hungry. Those were times when he did not want to eat and did not even think to go looking for food—either for me or for him. Those were hard times. As time passed and missed meals happened pretty regularly, I got skinny and often felt weak.

But I did not know what else I could do. Ned seemed to need me, and I needed him. My leg was slowly getting better but it still didn't work as well as it had before that car came out of nowhere and hit me. I could put a little weight on it now. But it tired easily. And when it was tired, it felt weak and shaky. Even on good days, it ached and I limped like an old dog. The other reason I could not leave Ned was that I had to guard him whenever he slept. Especially when he slept after drinking Jack Daniels.

Sometimes, when he was sleeping that deep, unnatural sleep where almost nothing could wake him, Bad People would come and stand over him. Once, a man leaned down and—keeping one eye on me—started to go through Ned's pockets. The man wanted whatever Ned had in his pockets, which wasn't very much, I knew, but still, the man wanted it. When things like that happened, all I had to do was growl and show my teeth. If necessary, I would stand up and let the fur rise on my back as I bared my teeth and gave a stern warning that I would follow up with action if action were needed.

My threats were usually enough to discourage anyone from stealing whatever was in Ned's pockets.

Eventually, Ned would be sober again. The whiskey would be gone and he would remember that I needed to be fed and looked after.

Once, when I got really itchy from fleas, Ned bought me a flea collar. He scraped together a few coins and rumpled old bills that he could have used to buy a bottle of Jack Daniels and instead bought me a flea collar so I would stop itching and scratching.

I knew Love when I saw it. Ally had taught me about Love, of course. And I still distantly remembered Being Loved in that Other Place I had come from as a helpless pup. Maybe My Purpose had changed, and now, I was to take care of Ned as best I could—and he would take care of me as best *he* could. We had been thrown together in circumstances neither one of us could control. I didn't know where Ally was—had no idea where they had taken her that night—and I could not leave Ned alone while I went looking for her. How would he manage without me?

So, almost without my knowing it or making any decision on the matter, Ally became My Dream. My Happy Memory. I snuggled next to Ned as we slept in alleys and under bridges—but it was Ally I dreamed of. She would always be my First Love, and I would never, *ever* forget her. She was everything that was True, Right and Good in The World—and if I couldn't have her, couldn't be with her…well, at least I had Ned. And Ned had me. Ned needed me too much for me to leave him.

But just I was getting comfortable and adapted, if not totally resigned, to this new existence, Life took another turn—a turn I could never have imagined.

CHAPTER EIGHT

The Worst Turn Of All

The days and nights were turning warmer. It was no longer quite so cold, so we weren't going much to the junkyard these days. We usually just slept wherever we found ourselves whenever we grew tired. It was evening now, and Ned and I were napping in a long dark alley at the end of a long day.

We awoke to find two men—dark, menacing shadows in the dim light of the poorly-lit alley—standing over us. I thought maybe they had come to search Ned's pockets and I jumped to my feet and stood guard over him, wobbling a little on my bad leg and because I had been startled out of a sound sleep. Still, I was determined to take a strong stand. A low grr-rrrrrrrrrowl rumbled thro   me and I tried to look as mean as possible.

"Hey, man..." One of the men nudged Ned with his foot. "This here your dog?"

Ned wiped the sleep from his eyes with one hand, blinked a few times and looked up at them. "What?" he asked. "What'cha want?"

The man nudged him again, a little harder. I barked sharply in warning.

"Hunh! He's a mean one, ain't he? Just what we're lookin' for."

"What? You mean Dawg?" Ned grabbed me by the collar and pulled me closer. "He ain't mean. He's just pertective. You lay a hand on me *or* him, and you'll be sorry."

"I ain't here to rough you up any. I just want your dog. I'm a Dog Man—and this here is my buddy, Raoule. We're both Dog Men. And you got the kind of dog we're lookin' for."

"You can't have him," Ned said, his fingers tightening on my collar. "This here is Dawg, and he's *my* dog. He ain't for sale, and I sure as hell ain't gonna give him to you."

"Raoule," said the first man, who wore black glasses and seemed to be dressed all in black, black jacket, black pants, black shoes He also had black skin and short, curling black hair, not straight hair like most men I had met. "Hand me that bag, will ya'?"

The man named Raoule—he was thin, hungry-looking and far lighter skinned than the first man—handed a brown paper bag to the one with the black glasses. Black Glasses reached inside it and withdrew a large brown bottle. "Looky what we got here," he drawled, but not exactly in a friendly manner. "Two big bottles of prime hootch."

Ned sat up straighter against the wall of the building near which we had been sleeping. He eyed the bottle Black Glasses held aloft with interest and let go of my collar. "Dawg is worth more'n that," he finally said, pointing at the bottle. "B'sides, he's *my* Dawg. I told you that already. He ain't fer sale."

"Well, what if we was to break this bottle over your fool head," Black Glasses threatened, raising the bottle. "Be a waste of good whiskey, and we'd still get the dog."

"Dawg wouldn't take kindly to that," Ned said. "You don't wanna test his good nature."

"Raoule," Black Glasses said softly. "Toss Dawg a little sample of what you got in your pocket. What you always keep with you, just in case we see a fine dawg like this one."

Raoule reached inside his pocket, withdrew something and threw it at me. It landed right near me, where I could smell it. It was red meat. A little off-smelling but still good. And I was hungry. Ned and I had been resting in the alley until it was safe to go looking for food. We hadn't gone Dumpster Diving for quite a while—maybe for a day or two. Or three.

I couldn't help myself. I snatched up the meat and wolfed it down fast before anyone could change his mind about my having it.

"Night, night, Dawg," said Black Glasses, and I could hear the menace in his tone, underneath his laughter.

Ned started to get up. "Now, just you wait a minute here! What did you give him?"

Black Glasses stopped him with a hand clamped onto his shoulder, holding Ned in place.

"Nothin' that'll really hurt him. But it *will* put him out like a light…. Night, night, Dawg," he crooned again, looking over at me through his shiny glasses. "And welcome to your new life as a Fightin' Dog. Put a little trainin' on you, and you'll be ready for the pit. And if you don't make it in the pit, you'll be Bait Dog for one of my champions, won't he, Raoule? Something for Bully t' sink his teeth into and practice his killin' technique."

"I said just you wait a minute!" Ned squawked, struggling to get to his feet. "I already told you—he ain't fer sale! You leave him alone. He's *mine*. You ain't takin' him nowhere."

Black Glasses raised the bottle of hootch high into the air over Ned's head. "And night, night to you, too, old man!"

Guessing his intent, I flung myself at him, deflecting the blow away from Ned and taking it full on the side of my own head. There came a terrible *thunk!* Glass shattered and pungent liquid drenched both me *and* Ned.

When I landed on the ground, my legs wouldn't work—not even the three good ones. I sprawled in a woozy heap, the world spinning about me, stars shooting past my eyes. All four of my legs were suddenly jerking and out of control.

That was the last thing I remembered until I awoke to find myself—stinking with whiskey—and locked in a Cage again, inside a dark building.

The only light came from a window high in a wall directly across from me. The window had a crack right down the center and the light was dim. It had to be almost the dark time that Humans call night.

Something heavy and cold hung around my neck and shoulders. When I moved, I heard a *Clank!* Clank, clank, clank....It finally came to me that around my upper body hung something far heavier than a leash or a clothesline or even the slender chain Ned had used to secure me; whatever it was, heavy lengths of it were wrapped at least twice around me.

The weight was such that I could hardly lift my head.

How had I gotten here? Where was I? Where was Ned?

I felt dizzy and achy all over. When I tried to move, the clanking noise grew louder, and my head hurt really bad. My heart turned over in sadness—and a sense of loss—as I realized that wherever I was, Ned wasn't with me. Like Ally, he had disappeared from my Life, and I knew that awful sense of complete certainty that I would *never* see him again. My Lost Human was truly lost, now, and once again, I was on my own.

I took a deep breath and tried to sort through the smells of this terrible place. Other dogs were here—in other Cages. I could smell them. But it was strangely silent. Other than an occasional clank or deep sigh, I could hear little sound. A heavy dark cloud seemed to fill the whole place, separating each dog in its darkened Cage, and weighing all of us down, down... down.

"Hello?" I whimpered. "Is someone here?"

I could see out of the front of my Cage, but not the sides. A length of something—a blanket maybe?—had been tossed over my Cage. It hung down on both sides and prevented me from seeing much of anything except the window in the wall across from me.

A low growling sound came from nearby. The growl told me to be quiet. Told me that whoever was growling would attack me if he ever had the chance. Dark energies were all around me, but most concentrated in the direction of that warning growl.

"What *is* this place?" I demanded, fighting my Fear. "What are we doing here? Why are we in Cages? Is this an Animal Shelter of some kind?"

At first no one answered. Then—from one side of me—came a voice. An old and tired voice. "Haven't you figured it out, yet? We're Fighting Dogs. We fight. That's what we do. We're in training. And when we're ready, they take us to The Pit where we have to try and kill each other. Last one standing wins."

"*What?*" I barked, incredulous. I did not believe him. "What are you talking about? I'm not supposed to bite. I can growl and warn someone away, but I'm not supposed to bite."

"Here, you bite—or you die. Your choice. You'll learn. They'll teach you. And if you don't learn good enough, you'll become a Bait Dog, and me or one of the other dogs will have to kill you...and we *will* kill you. Make no mistake about that."

"B-but I don't want to bite anyone. I don't want to kill. I don't want to *be* killed." I was suddenly frantic to make him understand. "That's not what I'm here for. That's not My Purpose. I'm supposed to take care of my Human—not kill other dogs. I'm supposed to Love my Human and..."

"*Love?* What's that? Never heard of it.... Whatever it is, we don't have it here. You'll learn. And if you don't learn, you'll die. I'll kill you myself when I meet you in The Pit."

"Not if I get him first," came that distinctive, menacing growl from nearby. "If they put him in with me, I'll take him down fast. I'm the best.

I'm the Champion. I can take down anything—and when I sink my teeth into you, whoever you are, I don't let go. You hear me? *I don't let go.* They'll have to pry my jaws open with a length of pipe to make me let go of you…. No matter. By then you'll be dead."

His words raised the fur on my back. I could not believe what I was hearing. What sort of Terrible Place was this? How had I gotten here? What had they given me that made me go to sleep so fast—and allowed them to bring me here without my knowing?

"Hush, now," another voice said. "Raoule is coming. I hear him."

Somewhere a door opened—a heavy door. I could tell by the sound of the door opening that it wasn't just a regular door. The man called Raoule came in and turned on a light. A bare bulb hung down from the ceiling and the enclosure now blazed with light. I had to blink to see Raoule. He had things in his hands—a long stick with a loop on the end of it, and a shorter stick, as well. Setting down the long stick, he took the shorter one and came right up to my Cage.

"Hey!" he said. "Hey, Dawg. You awake in there? You recover from your little snooze?"

He beat on my Cage with the stick, making another kind of loud clanging sound. "Wake up, Dawg. Lesson time. Time you learn some respect and who's in charge around here. Time you learn who's really Top Dawg."

Like my mother had done at the Animal Shelter, I cringed into the back of my Cage. My head still hurt and I was thirsty. So thirsty. I wanted— *needed*—water in the worst way. With the exception of that one piece of meat I had gobbled down, I had had nothing to eat or drink recently with Ned and the situation had now become desperate. My tongue felt swollen and stuck to the roof of my mouth. I felt dizzy enough to fall down, but struggled to stay on my feet.

Raoule flung open the gate to my Cage and jabbed at me with his stick, hitting me in the face and shoulders. I wanted to run out of the Cage but the stick was everywhere, jabbing at me and hitting me on the face, shoulders and nose. I could not move fast enough to escape it—not with the heavy thing hung around my neck and shoulders.

I couldn't bear it and growled in pain and anger. Raoule just laughed and jabbed me harder. "That's it, Dawg. Show me some sass. Boss-Man ain't gonna like it if you don't have no sass in you."

I growled again and lunged at the jabbing stick. I tried to grab it in my jaws. This made Raoule laugh even harder. "Yeah! That's it, Dawg. Come and get it."

The weight of what was wrapped around my neck and shoulders hampered my movements. Made me slow. Plus my head was spinning now. Nevertheless, I did finally grab the stick and chomp down hard on it. Only to find out that it was made of something cold and unyielding that had no give to it. I could hang on but I could not bite through it.

"Hah!" Raoule laughed, flinging me back and forth against the sides of the Cage as I clung mindlessly to the stick.

I crashed into first one side and then the other. Then I just let go. It was hard to keep a grip on the heavy, cold stick. And I was tiring fast. I didn't really want to fight and biting the hard stick seemed silly all of a sudden. Panting, I sank down on my haunches and looked at Raoule to see what he would do next.

He slammed my gate shut, went away for a few minutes and returned with a pan of water. I jumped to my feet, eager for the water. I was so terribly thirsty. I had to have that water or I would die. Nose to tail, I quivered with eagerness to lap up that water.

Setting it down in front of my Cage door, he sneered at me. "There it is, Dawg. But you can't have it. Not yet, anyway. Not 'til we get straight between us jus' exactly who's the Top Dawg around here."

He turned on his heel and began to bring water and food to the dogs in the other Cages. There were maybe seven of us, as near as I could tell. When he was done, he came back to me and adjusted the blanket over the top of my Cage. It had dislodged during my struggles just enough that I could see Cages of dogs on the one side of the room, all of them wolfing down their food while I was left to go hungry and could not even have the water just outside the gate of my prison.

I whimpered and begged for the water, focusing all my attention on it. Had I done this with Ally or even Ned, they would have known what I was asking, and they would have given the water to me. But not Raoule.

He laughed, leaned down, stuck his fingers in the pan of water, and then flicked the drops at me. "You want it bad, don't you, Dawg. Well, you can jus' go on wantin' it. I want you to want it *real* bad—so bad you can taste it."

I could already taste it. I managed to catch a few drops on my tongue when he flicked the water in my face. And it only made me thirstier.

Raoule took his stick and banged on some of the other Cages. "Hurry up, now, and finish. We got work t' do. You all gotta train t'day. Big fight comin' up soon. Lotta money riding on it. An' I'm gonna whip yore lazy asses inta shape if it's the last thing I do. Boss-Man says we gotta win every fight we enter...and we will, if Raoule has anything t' say about it."

Ignoring me, he went to one of the Cages I couldn't see, and when he came into view again, he had a black dog at the end of the long stick. It's head was caught in the loop and he could drag the dog after himself or push it away, whatever he wanted to do—and the dog would have no choice but to go or come, as he was told.

Why Raoule didn't just say "Come" or "Heel", I don't know. Maybe these dogs had never been trained as Ally had trained me?

Like me, the black dog had a heavy metal rope-like thing wrapped twice and hanging around his neck and shoulders. When Raoule got him under the light, he stopped, leaned down and attached something to the rope-like thing on either side of the black dog's head. The dog's head drooped and I could tell that the chunky black things were heavy, weighing him down even further.

"Carry them weights for awhile, you Sucker. Together with the heavy chains, them weights will build up your muscles. Make you strong in the front end. Now get yourself up on that treadmill. You got some runnin' t' do."

So the rope-like things *were* chains, after all. Just a different kind than I had known with Ned. But a treadmill? What was *that*?

In the corner, was something I had not noticed before. I didn't know what it was, but Sucker seemed to know what he was supposed to do. He went around to the back of this thing—the treadmill—and jumped up on it. Two elevated sides kept him from jumping off one way or the other, though he could have done so if had he really wanted to. But Raoule fastened him in place on the treadmill and then fiddled with dials and buttons on the top of the thing, and a whirring sound started up.

I was shocked to see Sucker start walking—and then running to keep from falling down, as the narrow floor moved faster and faster under his feet.

Sucker seemed to know what he was doing—how to balance himself, despite the chains and weights. Raoule kept him on the thing, running, for quite some time before he let him quit. When he took him off, Sucker was panting and looking very tired. But Raoule wasn't finished with him yet.

Before he put Sucker back into his Cage, he poked and prodded at him with the same heavy stick he had used on me. He kept poking and prodding and hitting Sucker until Sucker barred his teeth, growled and tried to attack. However, he couldn't reach Raoule because Raoule pushed him away with the long stick.

Raoule knew just how to use the long stick to hold Sucker away from him at the same time as he beat on him with the short stick. The more Sucker growled and tried to bite Raoule, the better Raoule seemed to like it and the more he would urge him to increase his efforts.

I had never imagined Humans doing something like this—provoking a dog to attack.

"Hah!" Raoule cried, jumping around in his excitement. "You almost ready for a kitty cat. You wanna tear apart a kitty cat, tuff guy? Ole Raoule gonna have to find you one. Or maybe I'll get you a bunny rabbit. You gotta learn to latch on and shake 'em to death. You gotta learn t' kill whatever's put in front of you. 'Cause if you don't kill it, it's sure as hell gonna kill *you*.... Hunh, Bully can tell you. Bully's killed so many dogs now I maybe lost count. Might be Boss-Man'll give you to Bully, if you don't get mean enough fast enough."

With that, Raoule kicked Sucker in the side, sent him sprawling, and only then dragged him back to his Cage to await another day of "training."

Each dog in turn had to endure the same process. First, the weights fastened onto their chains, then the treadmill, then the abuse and beatings. I watched as one dog after another endured the same routine.

When Raoule got out Bully, Bully was almost unmanageable. He came at my Cage like some wild crazy thing that wanted to eat me. He knocked over my water pan, spilling water all over and threw himself at my Cage door, snarling and trying to get it open so he could attack me.

Shaking all over, I retreated to the back of my Cage—but another part of me wanted to respond, to go after Bully and let him know that I would fight back. I wouldn't let Bully get me down and sink his fangs into my throat, as he wanted to do. I would fight for my Life. Such as my Life was—which wasn't much.

For his part, Bully was as fierce a dog as I had ever seen or met. Actually, I had never met anything like him. As Raoule dragged him to the treadmill, Bully made a point of threatening every dog in every Cage.

"I'll get you!" he snarled at each one of us. "I'll tear you apart."

Some of the dogs lunged at their own Cage doors trying to get at Bully. Not me, though. As soon as Bully stopped threatening me, I remembered my manners. This was no way to behave. Ally would not approve. Nor would Ned. With Ned, I had always practiced what Ned called "disdain" whenever we met up with other dogs. For the most part, I ignored other dogs. They were beneath me. Not worthy of my attention. I was on duty guarding Ned, and I had no time to make random acquaintances or get into squabbles.

When all the dogs had taken a turn on the treadmill, Raoule came back to me. Once again, he pounded on my Cage and provoked me until I barred my teeth and growled at him. He kept at it until I forgot all my good intentions and leapt at the Cage door, telling Raoule in no uncertain terms what I would do to him if I could only reach him.

Any other Human would have corrected me. Not Raoule. He laughed and said: "Atta boy, Dawg. There's hope for you yet. Big fellah like you, you could make a name for yourself in The Pit if you jus' get the right attitude. You got the head and the jaws for fightin'. Never mind that bum leg of yours. What matters is what's on the front end—and you got the jaws for fightin'. Question is: Do you got the will? The fire in the belly?"

So he had noticed my bum leg. Did he notice how thirsty I still was? I was panting, my tongue still sticking to the roof of my mouth. I needed water, and I needed it *now*. I cared nothing about—nor did I even understand—the rest of the stuff he had mentioned. The Will? The Fire in the Belly?

I barked at Raoule and backed it up with a long, low growl and a flash of my teeth.

Raoule snatched up the water pan, left for a moment and soon returned with it brimming over with water. I threw myself at the Cage door, eager to get to it.

Again, he set it down on the floor, dipped his fingers in the pan and flicked the water at me. "You gonna learn who the Top Dawg is around here, Dawg. You don't drink 'til I say drink. You don't eat 'til I say eat. And when I say fight, you damn well better fight or I'll get out the cattle prod…. Or maybe I'll clip jumper cables to your ears and hook you up to a battery. That usually works—if it don't kill you first. And if it *don't* work, I'll hang you up by your neck and let you swing til you either croak or learn to obey me. You hear me, Dawg? There ain't no other outcome here—you obey or you die. You *kill* or you die."

I whimpered and got down on my belly. I licked the droplets from my paws. I was desperate for water. But Raoule turned off the light and left, leaving us alone in the dark. Leaving me alone with my Terrible Thirst to think about all he had said—and all he had threatened. Cattle prods? Jumper cables? Whatever these things were, they did not sound good. I had come to an Awful, Awful Place—even worse than the Animal Shelter—and escape did not look possible.

Not possible, at all.

CHAPTER NINE

The Pit

Time passed in something of a blur, where it was hard to tell day from night, or season from season. I knew time was passing only by how cold or warm it was in the place where we were kept imprisoned in our Cages and let out only for "training." The jacket Raoule wore when he worked us gave way to a short-sleeved shirt that Ally had always called a tee-shirt. The tee-shirt hugged Raoule's slim body and revealed the muscles he had built up in his chest and upper arms, as he wielded the tools of training—the long stick with the loop on the end of it, and the short stick for beating and jabbing us.

Despite all the training, which unfolded day by miserable day, I did not really know what to expect at my first fight. I wasn't even sure I was going to fight.

When Raoule unloaded my Cage from the van, setting it down with a thunk on a thing with wheels so he didn't have to carry the Cage into a big building, he grumbled at me under his breath: "Waste of time bringin' you, boy. You ain't ready yet. Not sure what Boss-Man is thinkin'. Up to me, I'd have waited til next time."

If nothing else, I supposed I was there to watch and learn. Get used to the noise, the blood, the te   le sights, sounds and smells. Maybe I would have to fight—or maybe not. Once Raoule got me into the building—a warehouse, I heard it called—I was ignored and forgotten. All I knew was that there sure were a lot of dogs in Cages lining the walls. My Cage was up against a brick wall, along with the Cages of other dogs. As usual, I could see out of the front of my Cage but not the sides. It was a fairly warm night, but that had not kept Raoule from following his usual habits. The ever-present blanket was tossed over my Cage and hung down the sides, so that my view of my neighbors was blocked.

I could only see out the front of my Cage. However, I could see The Pit. Or at least, I could see some of it between the legs of the men who passed back and forth in front of me.

The Pit itself wasn't very big but had sides around it. I couldn't make out everything that went on inside it, but I could *hear* it all—and smell the blood, fear and sweat. I could hear the growls and the yelps of the dogs and the men's excited voices as they crowded around The Pit and urged on their favorites.

"Kill 'im! Go on, *kill* 'im."

Over and over, the men urged the dogs to kill.

And that's what the dogs tried to do: kill each other. They were supposed to fight until one of them couldn't fight any longer. If a dog tried to turn away from the fight, the men stopped the fight and the handlers or owners of the two dogs who were fighting had to get their dogs, take them back to what were called "scratch lines", and then release the two combatants again to finish what they'd started.

It didn't end until one of the dogs was dead or almost dead and unable to fight. The losers, if they were not dead already, were tossed back into their cages and left there to die of their wounds—and often, so were the winners. Or so it seemed to me from *my* vantage point. It was hard to tell exactly what happened to the dogs—winners or losers—except that no one seemed to be attending to them or trying to patch up their injuries. Maybe they were just left to lie in their cages until the night was over? I couldn't be sure. I do know that one dog died in the Cage right next to me.

I could hear his breathing—a wheezing noise as if he were struggling to get air inside him. And then I heard gasps and choking, and all of a sudden there was only silence in that Cage. I knew that the dog had stopped breathing altogether, and I could only be glad about it, because it meant that his suffering had ended.

No one would beat him any more or make him run on a treadmill or make him kill cats or rabbits—or string him up and leave him hanging until he almost died before they cut him down and sent him back to his cage to think about the experience of almost dying. No one would starve him one day and feed him big hunks of bloody raw meat the next day. He would not have to lie down in his own waste to sleep or smell the stink of too many dogs crowded into one place in filthy Cages.

All of these things had been done to the dogs that Raoule and Black Glasses managed. I had seen all of this and more during my time with Raoule—including dogs almost being drowned in a tub of water and then being "shocked" with a stick, the dreaded "cattle prod." The cattle prod jolted them so that they sometimes flew into the air and landed with a crash on the floor, where they jerked and twitched and whimpered, while Raoule laughed and kicked them in the belly to make them mean. To make them want to kill and fight to the death.

I myself had been kicked, beaten, starved, and forced to run on the treadmill until I could hardly stand. I wore the heavy chains and weights day and night. My whole world consisted of my Cage and my training. One day passed into another and I never saw green grass or sunshine. I never smelled or felt the wind in my face or heard one kind word. I could hardly remember anymore what Love was or how it felt to be Loved. Here, in my New Life, no one Loved me. No one cared. And what seemed even worse, I Loved no one. Instead, I learned to Hate. A Darkness had crept into me, filling my head, my heart, my belly.... The Darkness filled me and all the dogs around me.

We were *all* afraid of Raoule and Black Glasses. Oddly enough, sometimes our tormentors petted and rubbed us all over, as Ally or Ned used to do to me. It was as if they actually liked us—until they thought of some new way to make us suffer. To toughen us up and make us stronger and meaner, as they called it.

If I hadn't been scared enough before, I learned that night to be *terrified* of going into The Pit—that place of bleeding, pain and violence. Yet, in some strange, contrary way, I wanted to go in and just get it over with. I wanted to face my Fears and sink my teeth into the neck of my opponent and show the world that I was the tougher, meaner dog. All of Raoule's training had done its work. I was strong and I had learned to be mean. I was nothing like the dog I had once been—Ally's dog. Or even Ned's dog.

I was a Fighting Dog, now. I had been made into something I had never dreamed of being.

If I had to face Bully himself—the Champion—I was Ready. Even eager. I was tired of Bully's taunts and his boasting. I had had to watch Bully kill Sucker, who wound up being a Bait Dog, after all, because he did not take well enough to training. No matter what Raoule did to poor Sucker— and he did plenty—Sucker could not toughen up enough to suit Raoule. So he became a Bait Dog and died facing Bully. Bully tore his throat open and Sucker died making gurgling sounds that sometimes woke me from sleep long after he was dead.

Now, at the very end of the night, when the fighting had ended and the men were starting to load up their dogs and leave, Raoule and Black Glasses came for me.

By then, I was certain I would not be fighting that night. I thought we were just going to pack up and go home to the dingy, dark, cold place where we trained day after endless day.

It had begun to rain and I could hear rain pattering on the metal rooftop and smell the fresh clean scent of the wet night pouring into the building through its open doors. My nose had been twitching in appreciation, for the rain gave me something else to think about besides the stale smoky air trapped inside the warehouse. I had never liked thunder—and hated lightning, but tonight it was only rain—fresh and sweet and pure. Something I had neither seen, felt nor smelled since my time with Ned, which was so long ago now it, too, had become a Dream. Like my Dreams of Ally.

"Let's do it," Black Glasses said, bending down and peering into my Cage at me.

"Now?" asked Raoule. "Tonight? Hell, it's almost morning. And it's rainin'. We need to pack up and get outa here."

"Of course, now. Now's as good a time as any. Next time we come, he'll be fightin' for real. Won't be no practice or look-see session. Just hurry it up. I wanna get home before dawn myself."

Raoule hid a yawn behind his fist. He seemed tired and ready to leave. "Sooo, walk me through this again, Boss-Man. What exactly do you got set up?"

"Geezus. You're so dumb. Do I gotta spell it out for ya'? We're gonna put him in The Pit and give him his own Bait Dog to kill. He's gotta get blooded sometime. I want it done in The Pit so he knows his business when he gets in there next time we come."

"But where we gonna get a Bait Dog?" Raoule demanded. "We ain't gonna waste one of our own, are we? I put too damn much time inta trainin' them dogs to…"

"Nah!" Black Glasses cut him off. "I set it up for him to finish off one of tonight's Losers. Handler doesn't wanna keep the dog after it lost, now does he? Dog probably won't live through tomorrow, anyway. Better it serve as a Bait Dog for blooding *our* guy. You take our guy over and put him in The Pit and I'll go get the Bait Dog."

I didn't at all like what I was hearing—but I knew better than to object. So I was going to The Pit finally, after all. And I was going to have to kill my first dog. A Bait dog, not a fighter or a Champion like Bully. They weren't even giving me a cat to kill or a rabbit. I was getting one of my own kind—a dog who had lost a fight in The Pit and might already be dying.

Raoule yanked open my cage, looped me at the end of the long stick and dragged me out. I followed, knowing it was useless to pull back. I could not even imagine what he would do to me if I failed to perform as expected. If I failed to fight and kill as I had been trained to do, I myself would become a Bait Dog. After I'd been shocked, hung or tortured half to death as a lesson to the other dogs.

Thinking of poor Sucker, I shuddered.

By now, the warehouse was almost empty. Men in trucks and vans had been pulling into the building through its big open doors—or waiting just outside in the rain and loading up their dogs and departing. A few came over to see what Raoule was doing with me. I could hear him explaining in answer to their questions that I was going to be given a Loser as Bait Dog, so I could kill him in The Pit and learn my business before I had to fight for my own life.

All night I had watched Humans hanging over the side of The Pit, watching what was happening there. They seemed fascinated by the sight of one dog trying to kill another. And now, the few who had not already left started gathering again to watch me kill the Bait Dog, the Loser of his fight.

I couldn't help myself. I started to tremble in earnest. Whether from excitement, fear or loathing for what I was about to do, I cannot say.

But as Raoule scooped me up and dumped me inside The Pit, I almost peed myself.

The Pit was empty, but the sand in the bottom of it was wet in spots and darkly stained. My nose twitched from the scents suddenly assaulting me and I ran around, nose to the ground, taking it all in. Blood was everywhere. I could read the activity of the night spread out beneath my feet—where dogs had fallen, gotten up again, bled and died. Dogs had died inside The Pit that night. My nose told me so.

Dogs had done their Business—and not neatly, in one place. They had trailed it around The Pit. I smelled meat and innards. I smelled guts. I smelled death. The Pit was alive with scent. It filled my head, nose, eyes, ears and my whole being. I ran around sniffing, eating and drinking the smells, gulping them down, until the smells became a living part of me.

"Well," said Black Glasses, coming up to the side of The Pit with a dog in his arms. "There's not much life left in this little bitch—but she'll have to do."

Spotting her, I stopped and stared.

The dog in his arms was a female—smaller than me. She was what Black Glasses called a *Bitch-dog*. One ear had been torn from her head. One eye was swollen shut. Blood matted her brown and white fur. Long ripples of movement ran up and down her body. She shuddered from head to foot as Black Glasses held her away from him so his shirt would not be soiled. One of her front legs looked chewed and broken.

Her scent flooded my head and I quivered and shook. The smell of her blood made me feel a wildness inside that I could hardly contain. I heard myself making sounds I didn't know I could make.

Black Glasses laughed. "See?" he grunted to Raoule. "He wants her. Hold him a minute. Let him go crazy with wanting. The stink of the little Bitch's blood will send him right for her throat. He'll tear her apart."

Raoule leaned down and grabbed my collar. Black Glasses held the little female out in his arms. "Get a good whiff of her, boy," he said to me. "And then come finish her off. Rip her open, boy."

The little female's head rolled to one side and she looked at me with her one good eye.

She was almost gone, but I could see that she still knew what was happening—or about to happen. I growled and lunged at her, held back by Raoule.

By now, I was looking forward to this. I was going to do it. I would attack and kill her. Nothing could stop me. I was so strong, so powerful. My jaws would lock on her. I would taste blood and gristle. I would crunch bone. And she would die.

But just before Black Glasses lowered her into the pit and Raoule released me, the little female spoke to me. I heard her as clearly as I could hear almost any dog speaking in my head, speaking without words. Clear as can be, she sent me her thoughts in the way that most animals communicate with one another. I heard her despite the rain drumming harder now on the roof.

Just do it, she said. *Don't be afraid. You have no choice. And I'm ready. It's time for me to Go Back To Where I Came From.*

Her words echoed what my own little sister had said to me in an alley so long ago. *I have to Go Back To Where I Came From.*

Was I actually going to *kill* her? Go against everything my Ally had ever taught me about being a *Good Dog?*

Black Glasses opened his arms and hands, and let the little Bitch fall with a sickly thud into the pit. Raoule released my collar. I could feel the hair on my back and shoulders standing on end. A growl vibrated in my chest.

Yet I hung back.

She was so small and weak. So helpless. Black Glasses and Raoule and several other men near the pit shouted at me and shook their fists in the air, urging me to attack. The little female just lay there on her back, her belly exposed, her head turned in my direction as she watched me with her one good eye.

She was too broken to fight back—and too resigned to her fate. She had no fight left in her. She gave a soft little sigh. All I could think about in that moment was that she was Going Back To Where She Came From and she welcomed it. Whether or I tore her apart or not, she was leaving very soon.

Someone smacked my backside, shouting for me to get on with it. Startled, I looked up.

Above the dying dog's head and past the raised side of The Pit, I spotted the huge open doors of the warehouse. Rain slanted downward outside and cages were still being carried or wheeled out into the night to be loaded into waiting trucks and vans. The big doors stood wide open, yawning in invitation.

I did not hesitate. I leapt.

In two bounds I flew over my intended victim, scrabbled over the side of the pit and raced for the open doorway. Running as fast as I could—running for my own Life, now—I flew between men carrying cages or dragging dogs at the end of sticks—and hurled myself into the shadows between the wet black tires of the vehicles lined up outside.

I knew Raoule and Black Glasses would follow. They did. So did other men. They came running and shouting, trying to catch me or to block me. Golden light flooded the path to escape, silvering the falling raindrops. The beams from the headlights of a van in the driveway showed me the direction I should go. The van was one of several waiting to pull out into the street. It sat with its motor running, blocking anyone from shutting the huge open gates of the chain link fence surrounding the warehouse.

Tail between my legs, my body flattened to the ground, I raced through the opening of the big double gates and fled down the rain-washed street. Streetlights lit the way, but I sought the drenched black shadows, searching for the darkened alleys that I knew must be there, between the buildings. The rain pelted me but nothing could have stopped me.

A sound like a crack of thunder—the loudest thunder I had ever heard—blasted in my ears. Something whizzed past my head. It only made me run faster. I just kept running, running…. Seasoned by hours on a treadmill to build up my strength, even my bad leg had grown stronger and I could have run forever. I did run forever—or what seemed like forever. Up one alley and down another, running, running for freedom...

Freedom...leaving the men, the trucks, the vans, the Cages and long sticks, the warehouse and the pit...the awful pit...and the little dying female dog behind.

Far, far behind.

CHAPTER TEN

Freedom

Freedom is a wondrous thing. And a lonely thing, I was soon to learn. But on the rainy night of my escape, Freedom was all I wanted.

I ran until I could run no more. Gasping and wheezing, soaked to the skin from the rain but loving the feel of it, I finally staggered to a halt and collapsed in the mud under some bushes in an area that I thought might be a park. I had not seen a park in a long, long time, but I still remembered them from my long ago time with Ally.

Parks had grass, trees, bushes, benches, and places for small Humans to play. It had things called "swings and slides." Ally herself had once played on such things, though she wasn't a child. It was to a park that I thought I had finally come and I sprawled on the cool ground hidden from the sight of any passing Humans and struggled to catch my breath.

I knew that Black Glasses and Raoule would search for me. They never let a dog escape. They would kill it first. I must hide as well as I could. I could no longer trust Humans. Not *any* Human. Ned had not been able to protect me. Nor had Ally. Now that I knew about Humans who tortured and killed, who made dogs fight to the death, I must forever stay away from People—or I could be captured and kept in a Cage again and made to do Terrible Things.

I hid in the shelter of the wet bushes, sleeping and dozing, until the rain tapered off and the sun rose, climbing high into a bright sky filled with those puffy white things Humans call clouds . The day's heat warmed, dried and soothed me. People passed my hiding place but I was careful to lie very still, so no one knew I was there. I neither saw nor heard anyone who looked or sounded like Black Glasses or Raoule. I did hear voices, men and women—and later in the day, there were children, small Humans, laughing and playing in the park.

I could not risk leaving my hiding place until it was dark again. I grew miserably thirsty and hungry, but I had learned to go for long periods of time without food or water. I knew I could wait until the dark came before seeking either. The dark was my friend, hiding me from my Enemies.

When I slept, I dreamed. I dreamed of running, endlessly running… and I dreamed of Ally. I remembered our happy times together, the fun we had, the stories she told me, and her way of making me feel safe, protected and most of all, Loved.

Then would come the Fear again. And again, I must run. It was my running dream that woke me up. All four of my legs were churning, pawing at the underside of the bush beneath which I lay. The rustling noise woke me and I rolled onto my belly. Nostrils quivering, I tested the air for any nearby intruders. It was getting dark again, and soon I could go find something to eat and drink. I could run again…make certain that I was far enough away from Raoule and Black Glasses that they would never find me.

No more warehouses or dimly lit alleys for me. No more tall, crowded buildings where Danger and Bad Men could lurk. I must stay away from those. I must seek the places where I had known safety and Happiness— places Ally had taken me, such as parks. There had been one with a small lake with a sloping shoreline where I could easily find water. I remembered another near a river, though I wasn't sure where either park was because I did not know where I was now. It all seemed so long ago. It seemed like another lifetime altogether that belonged to some other dog, not me. Not the me I had become.

For food, I would look for trashcans I could tip over, since—without Ned—Dumpster Diving was out of the question.

Above all, I would avoid People. I just could not risk it. Though I had known Kindness and Love from Humans, I had also known Pain and Terror. Resolution rose up strong in me: *Never* would I allow myself to be forced into a Cage again. Never would I allow my Freedom to be taken away. I would starve first.

And as it happened—from that point on—I did starve.

As the days of my new-found Freedom passed, hunger became my constant companion. Sleeping in the park by day, I hunted for food at night. The hunt for food took me down streets lined with houses that had cars parked in driveways. There were alleys here, too, but they were different alleys than the ones I had known before, when I hung out with Ned. People put their trashcans out back of their houses in their alleys, if they had an alley. And if they did not, they kept their trashcans in their garages, where I couldn't get to them, except for every once in a while when they put the trashcans on the street to be emptied by men in big trucks.

Even if I could find trashcans packed full with trash, I often found little or no food inside them. I would tip them over with a loud clatter that sometimes brought someone running to see what was happening. I often had no time to investigate the contents of the cans I did manage to tip over. It became a daily struggle to find anything at all to eat.

When I did find something, I had to gobble it down quickly before someone spotted me and chased me away. And then I sometimes had to spend the next day hiding from the white truck that roamed the streets looking for stray dogs to pick up. I knew about the People in those trucks. They came from the Animal Shelter and their job was to capture dogs running loose on the street and take them away to Cages. I knew how all of that was bound to end, too. Those dogs would eventually be taken Down The Hall.

By now, I had lived long enough to know what was what. I had seen so much, experienced so much. The marks of my past—and precarious present—were all over my body. I still limped from time to time when my bad leg acted up. In no time at all—due to the scarcity of food—my ribs began to show through my coat. My coat itself became dull and itchy. I'd be doing something, sleeping or searching for food, and I would have to sit down wherever I was and scratch. It added to my misery and worry. What if I started losing my fur? Already I had some thin spots.

The days were still fairly comfortable but the nights were growing steadily colder. I knew that the Cold Time, what Ally and Ned had called winter, was coming eventually. And what would I do then, I wondered, when the snows came?

How would I stay warm? Where would I get water?

I had no blankets and saw no junkyards nearby where I could find an old junker stripped of its doors, crawl inside and huddle on a torn seat, out of the snow or rain, at least.

I began to be tempted by the idea of trying to find some Human who might befriend me and look after me, as Ned had done. Ned, I recalled with longing, had had blankets, which he willingly shared with me. He had sometimes built a fire in an empty trashcan under a bridge to help keep us warm at night. I had met him during winter but not that long after, the days had begun warming. There had been other men like Ned who lived rough and managed to survive. Could I find one of them to help me?

Oh, but I was still too wary and afraid to venture back into that part of town where men like Ned lived on the streets, and men like Raoule and Black Glasses hid in the shadows and stole dogs from their Humans. I didn't *really* want a homeless man like Ned, in any case, did I? What I wanted was someone who was kind, might feed me regularly, and might— dare I say it or even think it?—pet me or scratch my itches. Someone who would be glad to see me and not chase me away or shout at me. Someone who might even buy me a flea collar, as Ned had done.

But who could I ever trust?

Roaming the area in which I'd found myself after escaping the warehouse, I eventually discovered a yard behind a house where there was a shelter of sorts. Flat panels of some sort of wood were stacked against the back of a garage—a place where a car might normally be kept and where people often locked up their trashcans so I couldn't get to them. I discovered that I could wiggle into the narrow space between the wall of the garage and the flat panels of wood.

I found the spot during a thunderstorm. The thunder and lightning scared me so badly that I became desperate for any safe place that might be available. Bushes in the nearby park were my usual shelter—but they didn't keep out the rain if it was raining hard. I was searching for better protection when I happened to spot that narrow opening and thought I would try wiggling into it.

It turned out to be a wonderful shelter where the driving rain penetrated almost not at all. The garage's roof hung out over the top of the panels and helped keep the rain out of the space. And once I was in there, I felt safe and protected. I didn't think any Humans would notice me as I was completely out of sight of anyone passing by.

The space was dark and only just big enough for me to turn around in. If I were careful and carefully squeezed myself into it, it opened a little and became downright comfortable. Best of all, I could come and go as I pleased and always have shelter from rain—and eventually, snow, that cold white stuff that had so delighted me as a young dog with Ally but now filled me with dread just thinking of it.

This could work, I thought. If I can keep from starving.

Finding food remained the Big Problem. I knew the location of some promising dumpsters in the area but I couldn't get inside them. The dumpsters served restaurants and a place where Humans bought food and carried it out to their cars in brown paper bags. My nose often told me that food was in the dumpsters but knowing about it did me little good. I only had trashcans to rely on, and if I tipped over too many too often, the white truck would appear—driving up and down the streets and alleys. The Humans inside the white truck were looking for whoever had done the trashcan tipping. On days when the truck went slowly up and down the streets and alleys, I hid in my Special Place, sleeping the day away, determined not to be found.

It was on such a day that I was startled out of a snooze by the voice of a small Human calling at the entrance to my Special Place.

"Hello, dog! Are you in there?" the voice said. I jumped to my feet, prepared to escape in the opposite direction.

"I saw you go in there," the voice continued. "And I brought you a peanut butter sandwich just as soon as I could. I'll put it down right here. You can eat it whenever you want."

I peered at the shadowy figure trying her best to peer into my Special Place. The light of the late afternoon was behind her and I couldn't see her clearly. But I could tell she was a female. A small round face was looking back at me, her hair pulled tight into two twisted rope-like things falling one on each side of her face.

I saw at once that she was too big to follow me into my hiding place but also small enough that she could kneel down and look inside at me. Which she was doing now. How had she spotted me? *When* had she spotted me? I had been there almost all day.

"I live over there," she said, pointing across the alley to a house I knew was there but couldn't see at the moment. "I saw you from my bedroom window. It looks down on our yard and the alley. You went in there early this morning before I left for school, so I thought you'd be gone by now.... But no, here you are. Aren't you hungry? Don't you like peanut butter? Are you hurt? Why are you in here? Where do you live?"

The smell of the peanut butter suddenly reached my nose and made my mouth water. I had a memory of Ally sharing a peanut butter sandwich with me, and I started drooling as saliva filled my mouth. I scrunched myself together and wiggled around so I was facing her. Clearly, I should be worried that she had discovered my Special Place. I should leave by the opposite opening and run away before anything Bad could happen.

Just as clearly, I wanted that sandwich. My nose was twitching as I swiped my tongue over my mouth to catch my own drool.

"Come on," she said. "I know you're hungry. I saw how skinny you are this morning. Poor thing. Don't be afraid. I won't hurt you."

She pushed the sandwich a little closer to me. It was more than I could bear. I stretched out my body and inhaled its tantalizing peanut buttery goodness. Then I lost my head. I jumped up and grabbed it, wolfing it down like some distant wild relative might have done. Only too late, I remembered Ally telling me: "You mustn't wolf down your dinner, Jack. Take your time, it isn't going anywhere."

That had been long ago, before I knew what hunger really was—and what it could do to your pride and self-respect. When you are starving, you can't be polite or patient. You take what you can get before someone else makes off with it and you're left with nothing.

This girl-child could have changed her mind and snatched the sandwich away from me. I was just lucky she hadn't.

As I licked the last crumbs from my chops, the girl said to me: "I bet you're still hungry. Tomorrow, I'll try to bring you more food—and some water if I can find a pan to put it in. I can bring food everyday if you like. If you decide to stick around. I just can't take you home with me. I...I'm not allowed to have a dog. Dad says they're too much work and he isn't home enough to help me take care of one."

That sounded familiar; it was a story I had heard before, a long, long time ago. I lay on my belly watching the girl, noticing things I had not seen at first. She had a sprinkling of pale brown dots across her nose and on her cheeks. Freckles, Ally had called them. Ally had not been particularly happy about her own freckles, but seeing freckles on this girl's face made me feel as if she might be trusted—even though she wasn't Ally.

I lowered my nose to my paws and watched her—wondering what she might do next. She reached out one hand, as if to pet me, and I wiggled backwards, not sure I was ready for that. "I already told you. You mustn't be afraid," she crooned in a soft voice. "No one's going to hurt you. I brought you something to eat. You can trust me."

She smiled at me as Ally used to do, and I almost yelped in surprise. A Cage of silver wires covered her teeth. Each tooth looked trapped. But her smile reached even her eyes and made me feel safe. Her hair was a different color than Ally's—but she reminded me so much of her. This girl's eyes were the color of leaves in the springtime, her hair the shade of the sun doing down in the evening.

I decided to give her a chance. On my belly, I crept closer to her, alert for anything Bad she might try—like grabbing my collar.

But she didn't try anything.

Instead, she stretched her fingers toward me and let me sniff them. They smelled like peanut butter and bread. I edged a little closer, and very slowly, she lifted her hand and gently caressed my head.

It had been so long—so terribly long!—since I had been touched with Kindness. I lowered my head with a sigh that came from deep within me and let her hand roam over my whole head. Gently, she scratched behind my ears.

"You poor, poor old dog." Resting on her knees—she was wearing long pants, what Humans call jeans—she reached into my space with *both* hands and began rubbing my ears and neck.

"If you were *my* dog, I'd give you a bath and brush you and feed you and take you for walks…. I wish you *were* my dog. But I can't let my dad find out about you. He already called the Dog Warden about a stray dog that he said was a…a dangerous breed. I think he meant you. He must have seen you running around the neighborhood, tipping over trashcans. Or maybe it was Mrs. Grubowski who told him about you. I don't know how either one of them could have seen you but I guess one of them did."

She sighed and kept on petting me. And I kept on letting her do it. It felt so good. I hadn't known until just this minute how much I missed a kind and gentle Human touch.

"Daddy works all the time," she went on. "He's gone all day and when he's on duty at night, he's gone all night. Then he has a couple days off. He's a fireman—or a fire fighter, as some people call him. It's Mrs. Grubowski who takes care of me and fixes dinner and cleans the house—when she isn't watching her stories…. She's always watching her stories—her soaps, she calls them. Daddy doesn't know. He thinks she's always busy taking care of me. But that's not true. She doesn't even know I made you a sandwich and brought it out to you or that I'm out here right now with you. She thinks I'm upstairs in my room doing homework."

I listened while she petted and rubbed me and talked to me. Like Ally and Ned, she seemed to like talking to me and didn't need an answer. She just needed to tell me her secrets—things about herself and her life. Having just enjoyed a tasty sandwich, I found it no trouble at all to just lie there and close my eyes and let her hands work their magic on me. It felt soooo good. It felt so safe.

"My name is Bridget," she said. "What's *your* name? Or don't you have one? Since you're a stray dog—and a d-dangerous breed, like my dad said—you probably don't. Daddy said that there's a new law now that some kinds of dogs aren't allowed in the City anymore. He said that's why he had to call the Dog Warden to come and get the dog that was a dangerous breed. Which I think *must* have been you. You're the only stray dog I've seen around here."

She stopped petting me and leaned on her elbows, almost nose to nose with me. By now, she was half inside my Special Place.

"Don't worry, okay? I won't tell anyone about you. I'll bring you food and water—and a snuggly blanket so you can keep warm at night. But I won't tell *any*one that you're here. And when it gets cold—I mean, really cold, like when it snows—maybe I can sneak you into the shed.... We have a shed by the side of our house. Maybe you noticed it? My Dad keeps the lawn mower inside, but there's room for you. I just wish I could tell my mom about you. She would talk Daddy into letting me keep you. He would listen to *her*.... But...but my mom is up in Heaven. And...and she's never coming back. C-cancer, you know. Lymph—lymphoma. She got cancer and went to Heaven."

Bridget's voice wavered, and a tear rolled down her cheek. I was close enough to swipe it away with my tongue, catching it before it plopped on the ground.

Cancer? Lymphoma? I had never heard of them. But I knew they must be Bad Things.

When the girl—Bridget—talked about her mom and the cancer she got and how she went to Heaven—wherever that is—I could feel sadness all around her. The light and energy that was Bridget—my new friend—grew very dim. I whimpered and nosed her arm in sympathy, and also because I wanted her to keep petting me. Unless she wanted to go get another peanut butter sandwich for me; I would be perfectly happy to wait right here while she did.

"I think I'm going to call you Brownie," she said. "Because you have mostly brown fur. Well, you do have some white on you. But you're more brown than white. Would that be okay with you?"

I swiped my tongue across her cheek again to seal the deal. Yes, I would be Brownie. I would be almost anything if I could have peanut butter sandwiches and someone to pet me and whisper secrets in my ear.

And that was how I became Brownie, a Peanut Butter Sandwich Dog and Bridget's Secret New Friend.

CHAPTER ELEVEN

The Peanut Butter Sandwich Dog

That day began yet another New Adventure.

From that day onward, I stopped starving to death in that slow miserable way of stray dogs everywhere. Bridget became my new Best Friend, sneaking food and water to me every single day.

Often it was peanut butter sandwiches, because they were the easiest for her to get out of the house without Mrs. Grubowski or her dad noticing. Sometimes, Bridget brought me tuna or meatloaf or bologna sandwiches instead. Some days I had to wait a long time hiding in my Special Place before she appeared. She had to be so careful not to let anyone see me.

I got to know her schedule—when she went to school, when she came home, when she was most likely to be able to slip out the back door, cross her yard, step through a gap in the bushes that separated her yard from the alley itself, and come see me.

As I grew stronger from these secret meals, I had more energy. I wanted to spend more time with Bridget. I was excited to see her and several times forgot that no one was supposed to see *me*. If I trotted out of my Special Place to greet her, she would always pretend she didn't even know me. She would look around—setting off waves of energy that I knew to be panic—and loudly exclaim: "Well, where did *you* come from, Dog? You better go home now, you hear? Someone must be looking for you. You don't belong around here."

And I would remember the need for secrecy and play along with it. I would prance away from her down to the end of the alley and circle the block a time or two before slinking back to my Special Place to see what she might have left for me.

As the weather grew colder, it became more and more of a challenge for Bridget to sneak out of the house to bring me food. When she did bring it, her teeth sometimes chattered as she knelt on the ground to shove the sandwich or the biscuits or whatever she had brought me into my Special Place.

I still roamed the streets and alleys at night, getting my exercise and occasionally tipping over trashcans or going to the park to lap fresh water from a fast-running little stream I had found there. But I always came back to my Special Place during the daylight hours when Bridget was most likely to visit me—and also because I knew—having been chased numerous times—that I still risked being caught and taken away in that white truck to the Animal Shelter.

I had several close calls. Once, a man threw a brick at me and chased me down a nearby alley. "Get out of here, you damn Pit Bull!" I could hear him shouting. "Why haven't they caught you yet and put you down? You should be dead by now. You and your kind aren't allowed here."

I suppose I'll *never* know why People could be so afraid of me or why they hated the kind of dog I was. How did they even know I was a Pit Bull? How could they tell?

Whenever I met someone new—dog or Human—my biggest concern was the kind of energy they had. Was it dark and threatening, like Raoule's—or was it light, warm and welcoming—like Bridget's?

Sometimes, it was just...gray. A kind of nothingness, as if they could be either, given the right circumstances.

Try as I did to avoid other dogs, as well as Humans, sometimes I did meet up with one. After the preliminary circling and sniffing as we tested each other's intentions, I usually let them know I wasn't interested in hooking up. I would go my way, and he or she should go her way. Two dogs together would be easier for the white truck to find, and I couldn't risk it.

Plus, no way was I going to share Bridget and the food she brought. What we had was Special and another dog could ruin it. Another dog would almost certainly mean discovery.

And then one day, I nearly *was* discovered. Even worse, Bridget got into trouble because of me.

It was snowing—the first real snowfall of the season. A thin layer of the cold white stuff covered the alley. Hurrying home from the park, I was glad to duck into my Special Place and curl up on my blanket. I pawed it first into a nice nest, and then plopped down to await Bridget. She would be home from school soon—and as soon as she could, she would bring me something. That was our routine.

Except today she didn't.

I waited and waited, growing hungrier by the moment. She did not appear. Now, Bridget's house did *not* have a garage opening into the alley. Instead, the garage was attached to the house and opened onto the street, not the alley. The backyard had that shed for storage but it wasn't fenced, as were some of the yards. There were only those bushes along the alley side of Bridget's backyard, with the gap Bridget squeezed through whenever she came to see me. Before their leaves had fallen, the bushes had helped to conceal my hiding place in the alley.

Because I couldn't see the front of her house or her garage from the alley, I couldn't be sure if her dad was home or not. He always parked his truck in the garage, while Mrs. Grubowski parked in the driveway or out on the street.

I dozed while I waited for Bridget—but kept one ear cocked for the stealthy opening of the back door to her house. *Finally,* long after it had gotten dark, I heard it. Bridget was coming at last!

I jumped up in anticipation. What would she bring me on this cold, snowy night?

But before she got to me—while she was pushing through the opening in the bushes—her yard suddenly flooded with light and an angry voice called out: "Bridget! Where in heaven's name do you think you're going? What are you *doing* out here in the cold and dark?"

Bridget's voice, when she spoke, sounded muffled and thin—and very scared. "I...I...thought I heard a...a cat meowing, Daddy. I...I'm sure I did. I saw one earlier when I got home from school. It was...it was right near the shed."

"Well, if you did, you can't go out this time of night looking for it.... And why didn't you tell me? I would have helped you look, earlier. We could have maybe caught it and put it in the shed for the night—then taken it to the Animal Shelter tomorrow. You know tomorrow's my day off."

"B-but that's just it, Daddy. I don't want you to take it to the Animal Shelter. They won't do anything for it but...but put it to sleep. I...I just wanted to help. That's all. I wanted to give it something to eat. It's probably starving."

"Bridget, get in here. It's too darn cold to stand out in the snow, arguing. We'll discuss this when you get in here. Besides, you already know how I feel about stray animals. There are too darn many of them and the best thing you can do for a stray *any*thing is put it out of its misery."

"But Daddy," Bridget argued, anyway.

I peered out of the entrance to my Special Place. Through the gap in the leafless bushes, I saw her bundled-up figure trudging back toward the house through the falling snow. A tall man stood in the open doorway, shaking his head and frowning, his expression clearly visible in the light from the bare bulb above the door itself.

"But Daddy nothing," he said firmly. "Honey, you can't *do* stuff like this."

Holding the door open with one hand, he ran his other hand through his hair—hair the same color as Bridget's—making it stand on end. Then he sighed.

"We have discussed the matter of stray animals before, Bridget, and we have discussed the matter of pets. Now get in here before you catch cold. I can't believe you would go behind my back and try to feed a stray animal, young lady. I'll go looking for the darn thing tomorrow myself. And there will be no arguments about taking it to the Shelter if I find it. If it's out there, it's suffering tonight, anyway. Better it dies humanely than to starve or freeze to death. I thought you understood that by now. We've discussed all this often enough."

Bridget finally disappeared inside her house. I could hear the door being shut and a moment later, the light over the door went out, and the yard lay still and quiet, as snow continued to drift down from the sky. I shivered and crept back into my Special Place. There would be no food tonight, I knew...and maybe never again.

But I didn't count on Bridget's determination, even in the face of her dad's anger. It wasn't even light the next morning when I was awakened by a sound at the entrance to my Special Place. Brushing snow away with one hand, Bridget tossed me a peanut butter sandwich with the other. "Quick, Brownie. Eat this. And then you better get out of here before my dad wakes up. Go on now, hurry."

I didn't need to be told twice. I gobbled the sandwich, paused only long enough to give my sweet friend a tongue-swiping kiss on her cold, freckled cheek, and then I raced down the alleyway and headed for the park.

I didn't dare come back until the next day, after Bridget's dad had gone to work. Bridget came out of the house not long after I arrived home again and told me that Mrs. Grubowski had fallen asleep on the sofa watching her "soaps." Then Bridget fed me a whole chicken leg and three pieces of cheese. As I sat in the snow outside my Special Place, she sank to her knees and buried her fingers in my fur and told me what had happened when her dad came looking for the cat she had mentioned.

"My Dad found your footprints in the snow, Brownie. Of course, he didn't find any cat footprints because there isn't a cat. I lied about that. But when he saw your footprints—and *my* footprints, too—he got mad. He knew I hadn't told him the truth and it was probably *you*—a stray dog—I was trying to feed…. I don't think he knows where you hide exactly, but you'll need to go away for a little while, at least until the snow melts…. I'm sorry, Brownie, but I don't want you to have to go to the Animal Shelter. I know my dad will call them to come look for you. I just had to warn you…. Don't come back until it's safe, Brownie. And just remember, I love you!"

Bridget's green eyes filled with tears that spilled down her cheeks as she hugged and petted me. I whimpered and licked her face. *I didn't want to leave her.* But I knew I must, at least for a little while. I could hear her thoughts, not just her words, and I knew she was afraid for me and I had to go.

When we had finished saying our goodbyes, I tucked my tail between my legs and slunk away down the alley as Bridget stood sniffing, wiping her eyes and blowing me kisses as I left.

I knew I faced a long cold night trying to shelter in the park. And who knew how many more nights, after that?

But—lucky for me—the sun came out that very same day and the snow began to melt. The air felt warmer and by the next day, the snow was almost gone. I didn't have to worry about leaving footprints in it. Even so, as an extra precaution, I waited until after dark before slinking back—trying my best to be invisible—to my Special Place.

My blanket was still there, undisturbed from where I had left it. Best of all, Bridget had left me cold toast, two uncooked hotdogs and more cheese. Plus, an orange thing that Ally had called a carrot. I ate it all, even the carrot, which was not exactly one of my favorite foods. I hoped that the white truck had already come searching for me and given up. Not finding me, I hoped it would not return.

I slept deeply that night, glad to have my blanket, and knowing that Bridget wasn't far away. I would have to continue to be careful—*very* careful, but things were back to normal, now—whatever normal was.

Thank goodness, I'm a dog and not prone to worry as much as Humans seem to worry. Because little did I know that "normal" was not in my future. Instead, I was about to experience the most Defining Moment of my entire life—the one I had apparently been preparing for, although I had never known it, except in looking back on My Life as I am doing now.

CHAPTER TWELVE

The Defining Moment

In many ways, life *did* go back to normal, at least for a time.

Bridget and I continued as we had been—with her feeding and visiting me whenever she could. That happened every day, and often, even when her dad was home. When he *was* home, he was usually *busy*, as Bridget described him. He had to spend time paying bills or working on something she called a computer—which I already knew about because Ally had had a computer she spent time on. He also had to get lots of rest to make up for the nights when he got *no* rest because he was so *busy* at work. Often he had to go into work on his days off because they were "short-handed." Bridget's dad explained all this to her, and she then explained it all to me.

When Mrs. Grubowski was there, it was almost like having no one there at all. Mrs. Grubowski had no time to spend with Bridget, either. Her "soaps" took up almost every afternoon, and because she was getting old, she liked to sleep a lot on the sofa while she was watching them.

She did cook and do laundry and she cleaned the house, I was told, but she also expected Bridget to keep her own self occupied. She told Bridget she was sorry, but she wasn't there to "entertain" her. If Bridget's dad wanted "the personal touch", he should get himself another wife. Just because he'd lost Bridget's mom to Cancer didn't mean he shouldn't be out looking for a new mom for her by now. After all, the Bad Stuff with Bridget's mom had happened three years ago. He should be ready for a new relationship…or so Mrs. Grubowski informed Bridget, who then gravely informed me. Besides, Mrs. Grubowski was thinking about "retiring" soon, so she wouldn't be around to look after Bridget forever—all the more reason for Bridget's dad to get cracking and remarry.

All I really understood about *anything* was that Bridget was lonely—so lonely that one night, she came out to see me at a time I did not expect her. I only knew it was late, and I myself was planning on a little run to check out the trashcans a few streets away. Tonight was a night when People wheeled their trashcans out of their garages and took them down to the street to be emptied in the morning by men in big brown trucks.

I was just getting ready to leave when Bridget appeared at the entrance to my Special Place. "Are you in there, Brownie?"

I quickly went to her and licked her face in welcome. I would have licked her hands, too, but she had on those fuzzy things called mittens. It was, after all, another chilly night.

"B-Brownie," she hiccupped, and I knew she had been crying. Her face was wet with tears, her bright energy swallowed up by a big black cloud. "I had a bad dream, Brownie," she sniffled. "I woke up and was so scared. I couldn't go back to sleep so I went downstairs to wake up Mrs. Grubowski. Daddy's working tonight so Mrs. Grubowski is babysitting me."

Yes, I said, trying to comfort her and send her thoughts of sympathy and concern. *I'm here for you. It's all right now.*

"When I woke her up, Brownie, she just told me not to be such a baby and to go back to bed. So I did…. Then I got to thinking about my mom and I got to missing her and I felt so alone all of a sudden…and…well, I had to come out and see you. You're my only real friend, Brownie. The only one who understands me or really cares about me."

I'm glad you did come to see me, I assured her, swiping more kisses across her cheek. *You can come see me, anytime…. Did you bring me anything?*

No sooner had that last thought occurred to me when I felt ashamed of myself.

Bridget didn't have to bring me food for me to be her friend. I Loved Bridget. What I felt for her was very similar to what I had felt for Ally—and even for Ned. All I wanted was to make her smile and be Happy. I wanted to be with her forever. I wanted her bright warm energy to bubble up and surround both of us, as it usually did. If her energy grew dark and sad, I wanted to make everything right for her again.

"I'm going to sneak you inside the house, Brownie, and up to my room. Then you can sleep with me. You can come right into my bed with me, and we can sleep together, all warm and snuggly. Would you like that, Brownie?"

Well, of course, I would like that! I'd like nothing better. But…but…

"Don't worry, Brownie. Daddy won't be home again until the day after tomorrow. And Mrs. Grubowski will never know. I'll wait until she goes into the bathroom in the morning, and then I'll put you outside again. She takes a long time in the bathroom, you see. Hours and hours. And when she's in there, I'll just open the back door for you, and you can run outside quick and hide. What do you say?"

She rubbed her face in the fur on the back of my neck, and I could not say anything. Whatever she wanted—whatever seemed best for her—I would be Happy to do. If only she would smile, flashing the silver Cage on her teeth in the darkness.

I spent the rest of the night in Bridget's bed, the door closed on our own little world, all snug and warm, golden light shining all around us. That golden light was our Happiness, Bridget's and mine. I had not been so Happy since I had spent my last night in bed with Ally.

And the next morning it happened just as Bridget had told me it would.

Mrs. Grubowski, whose sickly sweet smell—old and not very fresh—was everywhere inside that house, started her day spending a long time in the bathroom. So Bridget had plenty of time to see me safely outside. A little later, before she walked up the street to catch the school bus at the bus stop, she even had time to sneak me a pop tart that I ate in a single gulp.

"See you later, Brownie," Bridget whispered to me behind the screen of the bare bushes lining her yard. "That old meanie—Mrs. Grubowski—almost didn't let me have that pop tart I just gave you. She said I eat too much. Said she doesn't know where I put it all; I must be going through a g-growth spurt."

I sat at Bridget's feet and gazed up at her, wagging my tail with all the Love and Longing in my heart. I wished that she and I could be together always…that I could sleep every night in her bed.

And that is almost—sort of—what started happening.

Whenever Bridget's dad was working and Mrs. Grubowski was staying over to take care of Bridget, Bridget would wait until Mrs. Grubowski fell asleep. Then she would come and get me. Pretty soon, I figured out that when Bridget opened the back door of the house and motioned for me to come to her, all I had to do was hurry over and follow her inside the house, through the kitchen, down the hallway and up the stairs to Bridget's room.

Mrs. Grubowski slept in a first floor bedroom and always closed her door at night. She never knew what was happening. She never saw us or seemed to hear us. Just as I had learned that I mustn't bark or whine when I lived with Ally in an apartment, I knew without anyone telling me that I must be quiet in Bridget's house. Not being a barker or a whiner, anyway, it wasn't all that hard. I was very quiet. But I could hear *her*—Mrs. Grubowski—snoring and snuffling behind her closed door.

Once upstairs, I stayed in Bridget's room with the door closed. There were two bedrooms—with a bathroom in between—on the second floor. The second bedroom was a big one that belonged to Bridget's dad. We never went in there.

There was another room on the second floor, where the door was always kept closed.

"That's the attic, Brownie," Bridget whispered to me one night. "If Mrs. Grubowski ever decides to come upstairs while you're here, I'll have to put you in there with all the boxes and bags and stuff. It's where my dad stores things he doesn't want to throw away. Some of my mom's stuff is in there. Mrs. Grubowski says we should get rid of it all—but I hope we never do. I like to go in there sometimes and look at it. Feel it. Some of my mom's stuff still smells like her. There's a blanket-kind of thing that my dad gave her for Christmas one year. She used to wrap us both up in it while we sat on the sofa and she read to me at night—when my dad was working. That's my favorite thing."

I nosed her hand and promised her that I would do whatever she wanted or needed me to do. My Life had found a New Purpose—and My Purpose now was Bridget. Keeping her Happy. Making her Smile. Helping her to feel Safe and Loved. After all I had been through, losing Ally, then Ned, and all the rest of it, I didn't know how I had gotten so lucky as to have Bridget come into my Life. She was now my Everything.

Soon, it was that time of year when Humans put up lights on their houses and haul big green trees into their homes to decorate. Sometimes, they put lighted or shiny things out in their front yards and fasten stuff that look like icicles all around their rooftops. I don't know why they do these things, but it's a Happy time of year, when Humans in general seem to have bright energy—almost everyone you see or meet. They smile at other Humans and prepare big feasts to eat with their Loved Ones. It was always Ally's favorite time of year and Bridget herself seemed all caught up in the spirit of it, telling me whenever I saw her what preparations were being made for the holiday she called Christmas. There was a tree to put up, presents to buy, lights to string on the front porch and over the garage...

But all was not as Happy as it *should* have been this time of year.

"My dad has to work on Christmas Eve," she tearfully told me one night after she had smuggled me upstairs to her room. "I *hate* that. I wish he didn't have to." She dug her fingers into my scruff and held her face close to mine, sniffing loudly as she continued her complaints.

"He should be here w..h me, but he said he has to work this year because it's his turn. He hasn't worked on Christmas Eve or Christmas Day since my mom died, so this year, we will just have to wait to celebrate until the day *after* Christmas when he comes home. Mrs. Grubowski is all mad about it, too. She said she wouldn't give up her own Christmas to take care of me unless my dad paid her extra for it. So he said he would give her a *bonus*. She likes to go visit her daughter and her family who live far away for Christmas—but now she has to stay here and take care of me.... Mrs. Grubowski *hates* me, Brownie. Well, maybe she doesn't hate me, exactly, but she doesn't like me very much, either. She only takes care of me because my dad *pays* her. She's not like a mom or a grandma—like other kids have— who just want to be with you because they *Love* you."

I burrowed my head into her side and tried to tell her that *I* Loved her, but she wasn't really listening.

With a sniff and a gulp, she whispered into my ear: "Why does every- one I Love leave me and go to Heaven, Brownie? I never even knew my mom's mom or dad; they died when I was really little. But I *would* have Loved them if I'd known them. And my dad has no family, either. He's been all alone for years and years—except he had my mom and me. But, without my mom, he only has me—and it's just not fair that we can't be together on Christmas Eve or Christmas Day.... Do you think it's fair, Brownie?"

I was the wrong dog to ask. To me, not much in Life was truly *fair*, when you got right down to it. So why worry about it? Sometimes it's bet- ter to just take Life as it comes and not worry so much about the fairness of it. There are good times, and there are bad times; this was one of the good times—for me, certainly, if not for Bridget, but I did not know how to explain all this.

All I could do was try and comfort my friend the best I could. I licked her face until she giggled and rolled over onto her side, pushing me away with one hand. Then she pulled me closer, wrapped her arms around me and gave a deep sigh. In a little while, she fell asleep, but I lay awake thinking about the general "unfairness" of Life. I myself had not always had an easy, safe time of it. And neither had Bridget. She had known Loss and Sorrow, just as I had. I had known Cruelty and Violence, as well.

I hoped Bridget would never have to experience things like that. I hoped that I could somehow prevent her from ever getting hurt or harmed—and that her dad would do more to help take care of her, as well. I actually found myself wishing he would spend more time with her, even though it would mean she'd be spending less time with *me*.

No matter how much I tried to comfort Bridget, she still needed her dad and the other Humans in her life to pay more attention to her, notice what she needed, and take care of her *feelings* as well as her physical needs.

Neither Bridget's dad nor Mrs. Grubowski knew about the tears Bridget shed all alone in her bed at night into my fur. They didn't know how alone she felt or how much she missed her mom. No more than they knew about the "dangerous dog" that often shared Bridget's bed at night, and gently as I could, I licked away her tears.

Goodness, but Humans could sometimes be so unaware of what was happening right under their noses. Could they not read one another's energy? Could they not look into each other's eyes and see the pain or sadness that might be lurking there?

Except for a precious few, Humans could not seem to read what a dog was thinking or suffering; I already knew that. Apparently—and this was shocking to me—they could not read each other, either. How sad was *that*?

I myself fell asleep soon after and thought no more about such mysteries until the night of Christmas Eve itself. It was quite late when Bridget finally opened the back door and motioned to me. I bounded up the steps and into the darkened house, and Bridget laid a finger to her lips: "Shhhhhh," she said. "Mrs. Grubowski only just now went to bed. I don't know if she's asleep yet. She insisted on reading me The Night Before Christmas, as if I'm just a little kid. But we had milk and cookies with it, so it was nice, actually, and she didn't seem so mad at me for ruining her Christmas.... Come on, Brownie. I saved a couple of cookies for *you*."

After she carefully locked the back door, we hurried down the hallway and up the stairs to her room. By the light of her nightlight, which she always liked to have on at night, she fed me two delicious cookies with frosting and sprinkles on them. Then she showed me something that seemed to make her very excited.

"Look here, Brownie. I have a Christmas candle. I found it in the holiday stuff in the attic.... Mrs. Grubowski said we couldn't light it and put it in the window to show the Christ Child the way to our house. She said candles are too dangerous and need watching if you light them. But my mom used to light this candle and put it in the window in the living room downstairs. Then we would sit on the sofa together, watching it and waiting for the Christ Child until I fell asleep in her lap. When I woke up again, it would be morning, and I'd be in my own bed, and Christmas would have come."

Bridget showed me a round chunk of something white that had green leaves carved into it. Carefully, she set it on top of a small cabinet in front of the window in her room. Then she pushed back the curtains that fell on either side of it.

"I'm going to light it, Brownie, and watch it all night while it's burning. Anyone outside will be able to see it and know that we're waiting for the Christ Child to come. I'm too big to believe in Santa Claus any longer— but I believe in the Christ Child. My mom always said He was *real*, and that if you light a candle on Christmas Eve and place it in the window, He'll know to come to your house and bring blessings for the New Year with Him.... Oh, Brownie! Do you think my mom will be able to see the candle from up in Heaven? And she'll remember how we used to do this together when my dad was away working on Christmas Eve?"

I knew nothing about this Christ Child or about candles in windows. But I was delighted to see Bridget so Happy and excited, when her dad wasn't even here for this night that meant so much to her and to Humans in general. I stuck my nose up on top of the cabinet and tried to sniff at the candle—but Bridget had put it close to the glass windowpane and I couldn't reach it.

Now, she was fumbling with a small box from which she took a little stick and began striking it against the side of the box. A light flared brightly at the end of the little stick and she very carefully touched it to the top of the candle where a second light flared. Then she blew out the light at the end of the little stick and wrinkled her nose at the smell of smoke that drifted from it.

I sniffed and sneezed when the smoke reached my own nose, making Bridget giggle.

When she turned to look at the candle, a beautiful light shone in both her eyes. "I think she'll see it, Brownie, and she'll know I'm thinking of her and remembering when we used to do this together. I had forgotten about this candle until I saw it—but no matter how much I begged Mrs. Grubowski, she wouldn't put it in the living room window and light it. She said, 'those times are gone, my dear, and you must accept it.' But I'll *never* accept it, Brownie.

Bridget leaned down kissed me on the nose. Then she straightened, her eyes glowing.

"Every year from now on, I'll light my own candle and think about the Christ Child coming and about how my mom and I used to do this on Christmas Eve. When my dad was home, we all did it together—but mostly I remember my mom and I doing it. I always tried to stay awake with her, but I never could. I couldn't stay awake for Santa Claus *or* the Christ Child to come. I always fell asleep."

I jumped up onto the bed, letting Bridget know that I was ready to curl up beside her and go to sleep, candle or no candle. It was bedtime— time to stop thinking about the past and enjoy snuggling. The candlelight did make a nice glow as it shimmered off the windowpane but I didn't see the point of staying awake to watch it.

Bridget saw what I was doing—curling myself into a ball—and she came to join me on the bed. "I have to stay awake and watch the candle, Brownie, but you can sleep," she said. "I'm not tired. I want to just lie here and think about my mom watching the candle shining in my window from up in Heaven. I *know* she's watching. I just know it."

Brudget's fingers stroked my head behind my ears. I sighed deeply in content and closed my eyes.

I don't know exactly what woke me—crackling sounds? The awful smell?... Or how hard it was becoming to breathe?

Suddenly, I was awake, and my throat, eyes and nose were filled with clogging smoke. A strange heat engulfed me, and orange flames were gobbling up the curtains at the window and jumping out of some books stacked nearby on the cabinet. The candle itself looked to be a puddle of something white and green, burned down to a nubbin and dripping all over the place.

This wasn't right. *This was terribly wrong.*

I nosed Bridget, fast asleep beside me. She felt hot to my touch and she moaned but didn't open her eyes. Smoke hung thick above her head and drifted over her body and the bedcovers. The flames seemed to be leaping everywhere and exploding in little bursts of new fire and smoke.

Hot air was blowing from the vent in the wall. This, I knew, was what kept the room so warm and comfortable when it was cold outside. The blowing air stirred the burning curtains—maybe it had pushed them too close to the flame of the burning candle?

I had seen the fire jump from Bridget's little stick to the top of the candle—and it was jumping now. Jumping from one thing to another. Soon the whole room would be burning. And we would be burning with it.

I disobeyed Bridget's most important rule: Don't bark. And I started barking. Or trying to bark. My throat was already so raw and sore that what came out of my mouth was more of a croak than a bark. So I grabbed the corner of Bridget's nightgown and tugged on it. She made another strange sound but didn't awaken—or seem to hear me barking and whining. Then she coughed. Choked, actually. I could hear her gasp as she tried to open her eyes, wake up, and breathe through the smoke.

I knew the exact moment when she began to feel the same panic I was feeling.

Eyes widening in alarm, tears streaming down her cheeks, she rolled over, coughing and choking, but couldn't seem to catch her breath. She was coughing so hard that she couldn't do much of anything except lie there hacking and choking, one hand on her throat, another covering her mouth.

This was too much for me. I knew she needed help to get up and out of that room—and the only Human around to help was Mrs. Grubowski downstairs behind a closed door.

I leapt off the bed, nosed open Bridget's door, which was not closed as tightly as usual, and raced down the stairwell toward the closed door that I knew was Mrs. Grubowski's. Jumping up on it, I tried again to bark. My bark wasn't very loud but I threw myself against the door and whined and whimpered. I leapt and scrabbled at the door, leaving scratch marks as I tried to push it open.

At first, I didn't think Mrs. Grubowski heard me. No noises came from behind the closed door. But then, suddenly, it opened, and there the woman stood, in a long white nightgown, her gray hair sticking up everywhere on her head, and a confused look on her face.

When she saw *me,* she blinked as if she could not believe her eyes. "What?" she cried. "*What?*"

Her jowls quivered and seemed not to know what to do. At least not until I grabbed the edge of *her* long white gown and tried to pull her down the hallway toward the stairs. Then she began screaming, as loud as I've ever heard a Human scream.

"*GET AWAY FROM ME!* What are you doing? How did you get in here? Where's Bridget?.... Oh, dear heavens, *BRIDGET!*"

I had her almost down the hallway now, and looking up, she saw the orange light at the top of the stairs and the black smoke swirling downward over us both. Thick, black, swirling smoke…

"Oh, dear heavens! Oh, dear Lord, no!" she screamed. "Fire! I have to call 9-1-1…. I have to get Bridget's daddy…. Let go of me, you brute!"

She gave me a vicious kick in the head and began stumbling toward the kitchen. But that was the wrong way to go. Bridget was upstairs alone with the fire. She wasn't *in* the kitchen. Didn't this crazy old woman understand that?

Her kick had dislodged me from holding onto her nightgown, but I grabbed it again while she kicked and screamed and tried to get away— dragging me along with her. When she got to the kitchen, she found the telephone—not a cell phone like Ally's, but one hanging on the wall. Quickly, she dialed and began screaming into the phone about the fire.

I couldn't wait to see if what she was doing would bring help. Bridget needed help *now.*

So I let go of Mrs. Grubowski's nightgown and fled the kitchen, racing back up the stairs.

The fire had spread; Bridget's *bed* was now burning. But Bridget wasn't in it. She was crouched in a corner behind the door, staring at the fire with wide, frightened eyes. Her tears had dried on her cheeks from the scorching heat, but I could still see the tracks they had made earlier.

Bridget didn't seem to know I was there—grabbing *her* nightgown again and trying to get her around the door and out of her room into the hallway. "Come *on*," I snarled. "You've got to get out of here. Come *on*, Bridget."

Bridget started coughing again. She bent over, gasping. The air was cleaner down by the floor; it was easier to breathe there. Only it still felt like we were breathing stinging hot air that any moment might burst into flame like everything else in the room. I myself could no longer see through the smoke. The crackling noise was loud in my ears and in my head as the fire gobbled up whatever it touched.

I could hear Mrs. Grubowski screaming. "Bridget! Bridget, where are you?"

That stupid Human. Didn't she know? Bridget was right here behind the bedroom door, too afraid to move, much less get up and run for her Life. I raced back toward the stairs, hoping I could get Mrs. Grubowski to follow me and help get Bridget out of her burning bedroom. Mrs. Grubowski was standing half way up the stairs, one hand pressed to her chest, her mouth open in a soundless scream.

I gave her an encouraging *woof!* to get her moving. It wasn't my usual woof, hoarse as it was. But it seemed to wake up Mrs. Grubowski. She grasped the railing and started to come up—only to clasp her chest again, swing half way around, and fall tumbling back down the steps she had just climbed.

Her face was scrunched up in pain and she was moaning and grunting. She clasped her chest with both hands and her body jerked as she lay at the bottom of the steps. And that was when I realized that whatever was wrong with Mrs. Grubowski, she would never be able to come and help Bridget.

Back I went to Bridget. This time I didn't just grab her nightgown, I grabbed her hand. I took her hand in my jaws, closed my mouth as tight as I could around it without hurting her and tugged. I tugged hard—and must have bitten down with my teeth, even though I didn't mean to. Bridget turned to me, suddenly noticing that I was there, her attention momentarily distracted from the fiery inferno crackling all around us.

I backed up, trying to drag her with me. And she suddenly seemed to understand. She tried to get to her feet but needed her hand, so I released it. She couldn't seem to stand up. So she crawled after me on hands and knees, following me out into the hallway. When we got to the top of the stairs, she stopped—and stared down wild-eyed at Mrs. Grubowski lying at the bottom of steps.

"It's okay," I tried to tell her. "Just go down and we'll get help for her. Just go down."

But Bridget started coughing again and gasping for air. She doubled over, coughing and coughing. I couldn't breathe, either. Black smoke now covered us, blinding us and making us choke. I thought then, that I heard sirens. Far away, but coming closer. Maybe it was Bridget's dad, coming to save her. To save *us*. Except he didn't even know about *me*. But he would help Bridget and Mrs. Grubowski. I had done all I could. I made one last effort to try and get Bridget to go down the stairs.

She stopped coughing. Now, she was just kneeling on her knees, hunched over with her head down, as if she could go no further. As if she were trying to get a breath of air but couldn't. I thought I could hear her lungs trying to work—to pull in air. But maybe it was just the sound of my own lungs trying to fill up. I don't know. I collapsed beside her and pushed my head into her side so she would know I was there. I leaned into her, letting her know I was still with her. I would never leave her. Never. Not if I died trying to save her.

And that was my last thought before the smoke swallowed us entirely.

CHAPTER THIRTEEN

What It's Like To Be Dead

Once I let go and surrendered to the smoke, it wasn't that bad, really. It stopped being scary. It stopped hurting to breathe. I felt as if I were floating somehow. I could look down and see both Bridget and myself, cuddled close together, my nose right next to her face. There was Bridget, and there was me—a brown and white Pit Bull covered with ash and wreathed in black smoke. Neither of us were moving. We certainly looked as if we were dead.

I could see Mrs. Grubowski, too, lying stretched out at the bottom of the steps, her hands clasped to her chest, her face wrinkled into that grimace of pain and surprise, her hair sticking up, her nightgown all dirty somehow. How had it gotten all streaked with black?

I wondered if we were *all* going to be dead soon, but I didn't see Mrs. Grubowski or Bridget floating beside me. They were lying quite still and unmoving. So I didn't know what to think was happening.

Whatever I was doing—floating above everything like that—it was like watching the pictures on a television screen. I saw what was there, what was moving, and what wasn't. But I wasn't a part of it. I was just an observer, watching and listening. Just so, had I once sat beside Ally as we watched her television—she had liked to watch something called football—without really understanding what was happening or going on. It was all just a world apart from me, something happening far, far away.

I do recall seeing—and hearing—the front door to the house come crashing down, and men with yellow hats, flapping yellow coats, covered faces and big black boots come rushing inside. They found Mrs.

Grubowski, and then saw Bridget and me at the top of the steps. But that's all I really remember.

Maybe I just floated away, finally.

All I know is that in the blink of an eye, I was somewhere else and saw a wonderfully familiar scene spread out before me—a scene of broad green fields and sweet running water. Blue skies. Warm sunshine. It was all there again, just waiting. Just waiting for *me*...and oh!

There was that *feeling* again—that marvelous feeling of being so *Loved*. So cared for. In that moment, I knew with great certainty that Someone had been right beside me all the days I had been living my Life on earth, without really knowing—or remembering—who that Someone was. Or who *I* was in this Wonderful Place.

Someone—the *Great* Someone—was *there* again, right beside me. Keeping me safe. Protecting me always.

I realized, then, what I had always somehow known: That no harm could *ever* really come to me, because this Huge, Enormous Love that had no beginning and no end, would *never* be taken from me...not *ever*. It was *always* here, just waiting for me. And wherever I was, it was always *there*, too—even if I didn't recognize it. Even if I was so busy thinking my own thoughts that I couldn't connect with it or *feel* it.

I was so tempted to go running across the fields again with my tongue hanging out—glad to be home and whole again. Thrilled to be Happy again—delighted to be where I *belonged,* where I had always belonged.

Yet, something held me back. I didn't see Bridget. She wasn't there with me. She was still back in the smoke at the top of the stairs, waiting for someone to rescue her. But—wait! Help had come. Maybe her dad was there to carry her out of the smoke and out of the burning house. It would be okay. She would be all right. She would *live*. It wasn't her time yet to Go Back To Where She Came From.

Do you want to stay? a voice asked kindly inside my head. *Or do you want to go back to Bridget? Whatever you decide will be fine with Me. I give you the Choice, Jack—just as I have always given you the Choice. When to Come and when to Go.... Every single thing you have experienced in this Go 'Round of Life has been your Choice...and this is just One More Choice you have to make.... What have you decided, Dear One?*

And just like that, I knew I had to stay with Bridget.

This place—the green fields, the sweet running water, the All-Encompassing *Love*—it would be here waiting for me. But Bridget, she *needed* me. I was her Brownie. If I left now, she would be so sad. She would not understand, no more than she understood that her mom was somewhere here waiting for her, waiting until she chose to come back. One day, she would see her mom again, just as I would see *my* mom again if I chose to stay.

Because, you see, Love *never* dies. And we are *Loved*. We are Loved *here,* on this Earth, and we are Loved in *That Other Place.* We are loved with a Love so *BIG,* so *ENDLESS,* we can't even begin to understand or comprehend it. The Love—the Energy of that Love—is just there, always was and always will be. Going round and round...*Forever.*

I did take a last longing look at all I was denying myself—for a time, anyway—if I went back to Bridget. And I felt a warm, comforting hand brush my head and tug gently at one of my ears.

Don't worry, Jack. I will see you soon enough. You'll be back here before you know it.

That was all I needed to hear. Okay, I told myself. I'm ready to go back now. I still have work to do. Something to do with Bridget. I'm not sure what it is yet, but I'm willing. I have a Purpose.

And that was all I knew until I woke up again inside a *Cage.*

Oh, no, I thought, opening my eyes and catching sight of the wire mesh enclosing me. Where was I? Where was Bridget?

Had I made the wrong choice?

Please. Don't tell me I came back to *this.*

I tried to lift my head and look around me. But I felt terribly weak and very shaky, as if I might fall down if I wasn't lying down already. My throat hurt. My nose hurt. My eyes hurt. My chest hurt. I felt terrible. Each breath I took was an effort. My chest seemed to be on fire on the *inside.* I wanted water—and I was hungry. But I didn't think I could eat a thing, not even if someone offered m⁓ *con,* which was highly unlikely.

"Dr. Carter?" a Human voice said. "I think your next patient is finally waking up. You know—that Pit Bull they brought in from that house fire? The one that saved the little girl and her babysitter, who almost died in the fire?... The one that was on the news?"

They're coming to take me Down The Hall, I thought. I'm in a Shelter. And I can't even stand up or bark at them. What kind of an end is this? I came back to help Bridget and they're going to send me Back To Where I Came From, anyway.

It all seemed so unfair.

"I'll be there in a minute," another voice answered. It sounded muffled, as if it came from another room. "So many emergencies tonight. Glad the dog is still alive. I wouldn't have been surprised if he died without ever waking up."

"Yeah," said the first voice. "The fire fighter who brought him to the clinic said he looked like a goner—but his daughter insisted we try and save him. She suffered severe smoke inhalation just like the dog did, but she resisted being put in the ambulance; all she seemed to care about was that dog. They were both very lucky—and the old gal babysitting the kid, too. She had a heart attack, the news said, but she's still with us.... Can you imagine? Having your house burn down on Christmas Eve? Almost dying in the incident? If it hadn't been for the dog waking up the babysitter, getting the kid out of her burning bedroom, making a racket..."

I just lay there listening—half drifting as they discussed what had happened. I felt so weak. At least, Bridget was safe—and Mrs. Grubowski. Neither had died. Bridget's dad must have gotten there in time to save them.

Funny. I could recall none of that. I had been...somewhere else entirely. Somewhere I could no longer remember exactly, except in bits and pieces...like memories of a dream I could not be certain I had really dreamed.

A few moments later, a Human female came and opened my Cage door. She reached in and patted me on the head. "Come on then, boy. Let's have the doc take a look at you. Frank, can you come get this guy onto an exam table?"

Frank proved to be a fine-looking young man with very dark skin, warm brown eyes and curly hair. He reminded me of Black Glasses, except his energy was completely different. I knew better than to be afraid. Carefully, he lifted me out of the enclosure and carried me to a table, where he set me down on a folded covering.

"There you go, boy," he said. "I'm honored to help you. You're a real live hero; do you know that? That's what they're saying on the news, anyway. You saved a kid's life. Got her out of her bedroom. Woke up her babysitter. Saved *her* life, too. Wouldn't leave the kid's side until help came.... Yet you're a Pit Bull—a dangerous breed that's been banned from the City. Wonder if your story will help change the minds of a few idiot politicians who put that stupid law in place. Gosh. I sure hope so."

This was all very interesting but I lay there, hardly listening. I was so very tired. Breathing wore me out. It was such a job to pull air into my lungs. I couldn't think of much else. I closed my eyes against the bright lights glaring down at me and struggled to keep breathing.

I sensed, rather than saw, someone come near me and bend over me. Then she was touching me with her hands, running her fingers all over my body. Her scent seemed familiar—but the inside of my nose was so raw that I could not be sure *what* I was smelling. Or maybe I was just dreaming, again. Dreaming of Ally as I so often did.

"This dog, " a voice said, a voice I *knew*. "This dog…I *know* him. His coloring. His markings. Dear God, can it be?…. Is this my old dog, *Jack?*"

My eyes flew open. My nose twitched. I tried to raise my head and really look at the woman bending over me.

No. I couldn't believe it.

But it was true. It was my Ally bending over me, stroking me gently, smiling through her tears. Blinking her blue eyes at me. Silvery drops were running down her cheeks to pool in her dimples. She looked different… but she looked the same. I would have known her anywhere.

"Jack," she said. "My sweet Jack. Is it really *you?*"

Somewhere I got the strength to wag my tail—to slap it hard against the table. I whined a little and tried to get up. Hands quickly restrained me.

"No, Jack. Stay. Don't try to move. You need to be treated. I can give you something to help you breathe better and to be more comfortable. You need to rest, now. That's a good boy. Just lie still, Jack. Lie still and let me help you."

And that was how I came back to life again…if I had ever really died.

I'll never know for sure, will I? Except I *did* go Back To Where I Came From—at least, for a little while. Long enough to decide that I still had work to do.

But what was I to do *now?*

I had thought I was coming back to take care of Bridget. But, here was my Ally taking care of *me!*

Would I have to choose between them? Did they *both* need me? How had Ally come to be here, anyway? Right when I needed *her.*

*Some*one had a sense of Humor—and was probably smiling over my new dilemma. I would have some questions for that Someone, someday. This was just too much.

Really too much.

Just when I thought I had everything perfectly figured out, here I was again…filled with confusion, having more questions than answers.

Grrrrrrrrrrr…

CHAPTER FOURTEEN

The Hero

Waking up to find that you've become a Hero is an unnerving experience; it's not for the faint-hearted.

As I mentioned when I began this Story, it does mean lots of adoring pats on the head and scratches on the belly. It also meant being confined to a Cage again until I began to feel better and to be able to breathe better. But of course, I didn't mind because I had Ally back in my life again. She was the one taking care of me in this place where sick dogs and cats came to be made well again. It wasn't an Animal Shelter, after all. It was an Animal Hospital—something very different, I soon gathered. Ally was now the veterinarian she had always wanted to be, having recovered from her own brush with death so long ago when I had lost her.

She had tried to find me, she told me in one of our heart-to-heart chats. She had looked and looked for me after she recovered and was released from the hospital. But no one knew what had happened to me. She had contacted all the Animal Shelters around but no one had reported a dog of my description being brought in.

She had even found a place to live outside the City where there would be plenty of space for her to keep me and let me run, if she ever found me again. But, of course, I had been having my own adventures, and she never had found me—until Bridget's dad carried me into the clinic where she now worked.

Another thing being a Hero meant was having my picture taken. I did not care much for picture-taking. It meant bright lights going off in my face and strangers exclaiming over me. Ally wouldn't let anyone take my picture until I was feeling better—but still, I didn't like it. And I didn't like all the questions they asked her.

"Isn't it true that this dog will have to be put down eventually, because of the City ordinance banning Pit Bulls and other dangerous breeds?" asked a picture-taking man.

I knew from Ally's sudden shift in energy that she did not like the question any more than I did.

"I live outside the City limits," she said, brushing back her pale hair and wrinkling her freckled nose. "And I will *not* let this dog be put down. But before *any* decisions are made regarding his future, I need to speak with the gentleman who brought the animal in here. I understand that his little girl thinks of the dog as *her* dog."

She was talking about Bridget, I knew. But where *was* Bridget? Would I ever see her again? She was "unfinished business." She was my friend. She was why I had come back and why I was being called a Hero. And I missed her.

And then, one day not long thereafter, Bridget and her dad were suddenly *there*—in the Animal Hospital.

Ally let me out of my Cage, and I ran to Bridget as soon as I saw her. She was all bundled up in her pink jacket, with a pink and blue scarf wrapped around her neck, and a pink hat covering her red hair. And she was wearing boots with snow still clinging to them. She stamped her feet and squealed when she saw me. I hurled myself into her arms as she bent down to embrace me. "Brownie! Oh, Brownie! I missed you so much!"

While we were hugging and I was slobbering all over her, kissing her, her dad stood behind her—tall and serious, his energy not exactly Happy but not Sad, either. I think he felt awkward, as if unsure what to do. Ally, meanwhile, stood behind me—and I suddenly worried that she might be wondering if I had forgotten *her* in all this excitement of being reunited with my friend, Bridget.

Breaking away from Bridget, I ran back toward Ally and bounced around her, then I raced back to Bridget, trying to tell them *both* how much I Loved them and how Happy I was that we were all together—me and the two Humans I Loved most in the world.

"Jack, calm down," Ally scolded, laughing in spite of herself.

"Brownie, calm down," Bridget said at almost the same time.

Then she stopped and looked at Ally, while Ally looked back at her.

"His name his Brownie," Bridget whispered with a lift of her chin. Then she repeated my name more loudly. "Brownie. Why did you call him Jack?"

"Because..." Ally softly began then stopped. Lifting her own chin, she continued more confidently. "Because I myself rescued him from an Animal Shelter long ago when he was just a pup. I named him Jack, and he was my best and dearest end—until one night when I got sick and an ambulance took me to the hospital. Jack ran after the ambulance, trying to stay with me. He got lost then, and I could never find him. I thought he was probably dead—until your dad brought him into the clinic after he saved you from the fire."

"Oh," said Bridget in a small, lost voice. She scuffed at the floor with one boot and took her dad's hand. "You mean he's really *your* dog—and he can't be *my* dog? Even though I found him starving in the ally and I took care of him? My dad says that since Brownie saved my life—and I love him so much—that we'll try and find a way to keep him. He deserves a home with someone who loves him as much as I do."

"Yes, he does," said Ally bending down to scratch behind my ears. "And I think we should all discuss this—because Jack—Brownie, as you call him—can't live in the City. He's not allowed to be here, even now. Even though he's a Hero. *You* live in the City, don't you?"

Ally straightened from petting me and looked at Bridget's dad, who solemnly nodded.

Bridget's dad was *very* tall, I noticed, now that I could see him up close—a fine specimen of a Human, with gentle eyes and an understanding face with no anger in it, only something that I thought might be regret. He had the same red hair and green eyes as Bridget, the same mouth, too, and it was turned down at the corners.

"We do live in the City," he said. "And I plan to fight that City ordinance banning *supposedly* dangerous breeds of dogs and get it changed. If it weren't for *this* dog, this Pit Bull who has been sleeping in my daughter's bed and looking after her when I wasn't there—if it weren't for *him*—she would be dead, now. And so would Mrs. Grubowski, her babysitter."

He reached down to pat my head and I liked how his hand felt. I liked his energy. And immediately started to regret all the bad thoughts I had had about him in the past and how quickly I had judged him.

"This dog truly *is* a Hero," he continued. "And I'm here to tell you that I won't let him be put down, no matter what *any*one says. The entire Fire Department is going to petition the City Council to change the ordinance banning dangerous breeds. If the City wants to do something to keep people from getting bit by dogs, they need to start dealing with Bad Owners who mistreat and don't train their dogs properly, so they're *not* dangerous to People. We're going to change things, Doc, so that Brownie *can* live with *us*."

"Really," said Ally, looking him up and down, her eyes sparkling with approval, but still somewhat doubtful. "That's a fine plan. But it will take time to change an ordinance and Jack—Brownie—needs to be removed from the Animal Hospital to somewhere safe outside the City until that can happen."

"Yes, well…" Bridget's dad began again, but Ally held up one hand.

"There's also the matter of Jack actually being *my* dog and I *do* live outside the City limits, where the ordinance cannot affect him."

Bridget's eyes suddenly welled with tears. "But…but if *you* take him, I…I'll never get to see him again, will I?"

Bridget dropped to her knees on the floor of the clinic. Snow was now melting and making a puddle near her boots. She didn't seem to notice. She opened her arms to me and I bounded into them, licking her face in joy that she was actually here with me. "I love you, Brownie," she wailed. "I love you so much!"

Over our heads, Bridget's dad and my Ally seemed to be staring at one another and shaking *their* heads.

"It seems," Ally said. "That we have a problem, don't we?"

"Yes," Bridget's dad agreed. "It would seem so. Would it be too much to ask if we could find some way to get the two of them—Brownie—Jack—and Bridget together occasionally for visits? I mean, while we figure out who gets to keep this dog, eventually? That is, if your husband wouldn't mind such an arrangement."

"Oh, I'm not married," said Ally. "I live alone when I'm not working day and night at the clinic. Jack can stay with me while you're getting that ordinance repealed, and Bridget is welcome to come visit him anytime— especially on weekends, if that works for you. And once the ordinance no longer poses a problem—if that happens—we can discuss a more permanent arrangement."

She tilted her head and watched Bridget's dad carefully. "However, I warn you; I love this dog, too. He saved *me* way back when—when someone was trying to hurt *me*. I dimly recall him chasing away a bad guy bent on doing me harm—and then he got help for me, much as he did for Bridget when *she* needed help. Or so I was told."

Ally smiled then at Bridget's dad—and tears glimmered in her sky-blue eyes. "Whether we call him Brownie—or Jack—he's a *very* special dog. I can't just say goodbye to him and give him up. Not now, when I've found him again. You understand, don't you?"

Bridget's dad could not seem to look away from Ally. Their gazes had locked together, as if they were looking into each other's hearts, not just into each other's eyes. The very air in the clinic quivered with intense energy—yet I sensed that it was a *good* energy, not a bad one.

"Yes," he finally said, nodding and resting one hand atop Bridget's head. "I do understand that. This is a dog who loves unconditionally and puts the ones he loves ahead of himself and his own safety. You can't ask for more than that from *any*one. Certainly, there's no finer dog anywhere. As I said, he's a true Hero."

"Maybe we should change his name to Hero," said Ally, bursting into laughter. "It would certainly fit him."

"No," Bridget piped up. "If you named him Jack when he was a puppy, then his name is really Jack, not Brownie or Hero. And if *you* love him as much as I do, then we *have* to share him somehow, don't we, Dad?"

Bridget tugged on her dad's hand. "You'll take me to see him every weekend, won't you, Daddy? You promise? Except maybe for the weekends you have to work—and then you'll take me after school, maybe?"

"Will that be too often—us coming out to your place that much?" Bridget's dad asked Ally. "We don't want to impose."

"If I can't manage it for any reason, I'll let you know." Ally's smile lit up her face, deepening her dimples. "We'll have to try it and see, won't we?"

And so they did.

And that was how I became The Happiest Dog In The World.

CHAPTER FIFTEEN

The Happiest Dog In The World

Going home with Ally—living with her outside the City limits in an old farmhouse—was a lot like returning to That Other Place. Except for the snow on the ground, of course. Even with the snow, I could tell that this was a place of fields that would be green again very soon. It was a place of trees, with a patch of woods nearby, and a frozen "creek", as Ally called it. It was place for a dog to run and be Happy—and I was living here with Ally. Best of all, I got to see Bridget a *lot.*

She came almost every weekend—or at least every week. As winter gave way to springtime, green grass grew, and leaves unfurled on the trees again. It seemed like Heaven to all of us. Ally, Bridget and her dad, and I took to taking long walks down the country road or in the patch of woods.

We grilled hamburgers outside and hot dogs when the weather was nice—and stayed inside and made hot chocolate when it was not. My Humans played board games on the kitchen table while I sat under it nosing first one foot, then the other, just to assure myself that everyone I cared about was here, hanging out with me—laughing and talking and having a wonderful time together.

Well, anyone could guess what was bound to happen—I believe Humans call it *romance.*

Ally and Bridget's dad began to want to spend more and more time together. Not just because of me and Bridget—but because they liked each other so much. If Bridget fell asleep on the sofa because they stayed so late on a Saturday night, Bridget's dad and my Ally liked to kiss, hug and hold each other, and talk about the Future. I sometimes nosed my way in between them because I wanted attention—and because I loved the energy that surrounded them, as they looked deep into each other's eyes. They could not keep their hands to themselves but I wanted them to pet *me,* not each other. They were so Happy, the way Humans are *meant* to be!

It made *me* so Happy, too, and Bridget even Happier.

When they weren't hugging and kissing, they talked about everything and nothing. They especially liked to talk about how the City ordinance had been so easily overturned after an article—and my picture—appeared in the City newspaper. The article pointed out how wonderful and heroic Pit Bulls can be, and how we are really marvelous family dogs if given half a chance.

Not long after the article appeared, dog owners of all sorts, accompanied by all of the City's fire fighters who weren't on duty at the time, stormed City Council chambers demanding that the ordinance be repealed.

And it was.

A new ordinance was then passed that *cracked down,* as Bridget's dad called it, on dog fighting and made it a serious crime to be abusive to animals or to neglect them, both dogs and cats. Ally and Bridget's dad helped make all of this happen. Ally brought the dog owners—Responsible Owners, she called them—and veterinarians together, and Bridget's dad organized the Fire Department. The rest, as Humans say, was History.

It became a perfect example of how Humans working together, side by side, can *make things happen for the better.*

I can't quite understand, though, why it took so long for folks to realize that there really are *no* Bad Dogs, just as there are *no* Bad Humans. There are only dogs—and Humans—who *behave* badly because they have been *treated* badly when too young and tender to defend themselves, or to realize that Life *can* and *should* be different.

We can become Sick inside our heads, somehow, and we can be very *confused* about what's Right or Wrong—but Badness isn't *bred* into either of our species; it is not who we *are*. It is only who we become when we ourselves are treated badly.

At least, that's *my* opinion.

Bully—the Champion Fighting Dog who was taught to kill anything put in front of him—could have told the City Council all this. He was Living Proof. I myself could have told them, but I guess My Story was what convinced them, finally—and I am so thankful it did.

When my Ally and Bridget's dad finally "tied the knot," whatever that means, I got to be Flower Dog. This meant I was supposed to follow Bridget, who was Ring Bearer, down the aisle of the little church where Ally and Bridget's dad tied that knot.

Not so hard you might think, to be a Flower Dog, especially now that I was "legal," my breed no longer banned from appearing in public. But try carrying a basket of flowers by its handle in your mouth while you are trotting down the aisle—and everyone in the pews is reaching out to pet you as you pass.

I was glad when it was over, and I could take up my position near the food table at the party afterwards. The celebration was held at Ally's house, where Bridget and her dad had decided to live with Ally—all of them together—in our Heavenly Place…. And oh, it was a grand party!

The most delicious little meatballs—and chicken!—were on the menu. All I had to do was sit quietly, tilt my head and send out pleading thoughts, and folks usually obliged me with a tidbit—if Ally and Bridget were not looking in my direction.

Both were determined to keep me from getting sick eating things I shouldn't have, plus they frowned on my begging. Ally had taught Bridget a great deal about the proper feeding, care, and discipline of dogs, and as a result, Bridget had become much stricter with me. Still loving, still my best friend, but now also determined that I should be well behaved and looked after, just as Ally herself insisted upon, Bridget was becoming *very* strict.

No more sugar cookies with icing and sprinkles. No more pop tarts. By now, Bridget had decided that she, too, wanted to be a veterinarian when she grew up.

Though I loved to silently beg from unsuspecting guests, I never argued with my Humans, when they said no to something I wanted. I was, after all, a Good Dog, and knew better than to disobey. (Well, other than that little misadventure involving roast beef that Bridget's dad left right under my nose.)

Hero or not, I was only permitted Special Treats on occasion, and *after* I had earned them. Only once in a very great while was I granted my *favorite* Special Treat of all time—*bacon*.

And so time passed. Soon, I had a little boy to look after—just as I had been looking after Bridget. His name was Justin, and as he grew, he loved to yank on my ears when no one was looking, fall asleep while lying on top of me, and take food right out of my mouth if he could grab it. He would then eat it himself. When he awoke lonely in the night, I jumped into bed with him and kept him company. I made him laugh and helped him get his exercise tossing balls to me. I was right there when he took his first steps and when he took his first bike ride. When he fell down and scraped his knees or bloodied his nose, I licked away the tears and the blood, (Can you hear Bridget saying "Eeew!) and made him laugh again.

This is what dogs do, after all. This is our job. We look after our Humans. If they get too Serious, we make them Smile. If they get too Sad, we lap away their tears. If they get too "Busy", we remind them that Life is for Living, Laughing and Taking Long Walks, whatever the weather.

Humans like to live in their heads, you see. That's where they spend far too much time worrying about the Past and Future. But we dogs live in the *NOW*. We notice and respond to everything we see, smell or hear.

We are *here* for our Humans. What makes us Happy is when our Humans remember to put down their cell phones or their computers, stop thinking unnecessary, worrisome thoughts, and be *here* and now for *us*.

We *love* Life and we live it fully. I guess you could say we are *all* Heroes, of one sort or another. When we love our Humans, we give our lives for them in a hundred thousand little ways, large and small, day after day.

Of course, even Heroes get old.

My muzzle has now gone gray. Silver hairs sprout in odd places, like on my eyebrows, for goodness sake.

Bridget is rarely home any more because she is busy with her studies, so she can one day become a veterinarian like my Ally. Justin races off all the time to play sports—and the new Little One in the house is hardly big enough to want to play with me yet. Her name is Emily.

She may be small but her yell is mighty. And sometimes, she *smells* quite pungently. She deposits in her pants what I only do outside on the grass. I spend most of my time these days looking after her, letting Ally know when she needs something—like her pants changed.

Except when my joints ache and I don't feel too well or too energetic.

On such days, Ally lets me go into her bedroom and then shuts the door after me, and allows me to rest on her bed by myself, where the cats can't get to me.

Yes, we have three cats, now—a black one, an orange one and a gray one. All of them are Rescue Cats, so you would think they'd be more grateful and accommodating—but no. They seem to think they own the place and one of their favorite things is to bother me when I am trying to sleep. They learned as kittens to pounce on me unexpectedly, so I would "Woof!" in surprise, which apparently strikes them as being hilarious.

That said, I don't mind them so much in the winter when we sometimes curl up together in front of the fireplace to snooze while keeping cozy. Those times can be rather nice, actually.

Recently, we acquired another Pit Bull—a puppy named Clown. He is all white in color with a black ring around one eye. He's having trouble getting Housebroken, so he spends a lot of time out on the enclosed porch. Once he's allowed inside more, I'll have much to teach him—if he's willing to listen, which I doubt, him being a Crazy Undisciplined Puppy.

The few times I've tried to correct him or tell him what's what, he never listens. His mind is somewhere else—he's trying to chew on something or he's tumbling all over his own feet, getting into mischief. But, I expect he'll learn in time why he's here and what his job is. We each have to learn this stuff in our own good time at our own pace.

Sometimes, when my joints are aching *really* bad, Ally rubs me down and then gives me medicine to help me feel better. She sighs and gets all weepy, saying things like: "You are getting so old, Jack. So old and creaky. What will I ever do without you? How will I find the strength to do what must be done, when the time comes?"

I'm not worried. Ally will take care of me. She will not let me suffer. When the time comes, she will gently help me to Go Back To Where I Came From while I still have my dignity and before I suffer too much. And when I go—when I leave my Family behind—I know it will be okay. It will be fine. It will be just as it should be.

You see I know what is awaiting me there. And I know I will never really leave the ones I Love. We may be parted for a time, but—eventually—we will all be together again in that Wonderful Other Place—our One True Home, where Love surrounds us. Where Love fills us with such Beauty and Endless Joy that all of our days shimmer with Golden Light. There is no Sorrow there, and no unhappiness. There are no Goodbyes.

I don't know why Humans get so choked up, so sad or scared about the thought of Going Back To Where We Come From.

Sometimes, I can hardly wait.

The *Great Someone* is awaiting me there—and His pockets!

Oh, His pockets are full of *bacon*.

When my Humans return to That Other Place, His pockets will be full of whatever bacon means to *them*. Just like me, they will have an endless supply of whatever they need to be Happy. That's what will be awaiting *them*—Love and bacon, as much as they could ever want or desire.

And me. *I* will be awaiting them. I will greet them with slobbery kisses!

And so I must end My Story.

I'm feeling weary and must leave you now and go take a nap.

Besides, I've told you My Story—everything I know about why I came here and what happened to me.

Whether you believe it or not is entirely up to you. Makes no difference if you believe it, or if you don't. It's all the same to me. After years of uncertainty, confusion and doubt, I've finally figured Everything out.

I know who I am, finally…

I am Jack, the Pit Bull.

I'm just a dog, though I've heard Humans say that Dog means God spelled backward.

Well, I'm certainly not God and I can't take credit for making *that* up. (Even though I'm secretly flattered. I may be an Old Dog but I still enjoy flattery. *God*, huh? Well…ah…ahem, maybe just a *little* bit…)

I only know I'm here because the *Great Someone* sent me—or, rather, gave me the chance to come here if I wanted. I've come and I've lived My Purpose, which is all any of us can ever hope to do. If we live Our Purpose—we can Go Back To Where We Came From with No Regrets.

We will know we have done Our Best—and we *deserve* to be rewarded.

Don't you think so?

(Bacon, here I come!)

Until we meet again,

Your Devoted Friend and Teacher,
Jack
The Pit Bull who became a Hero.

Some Facts About Pit Bulls:

The term "Pit Bull" or pitbull, is actually a catch-all term that applies to several breeds of dogs. The following are all recognized as Pit Bulls, despite distinct, differing characteristics and even appearances:

American Pit Bull Terrier

American Bulldog

American Staffordshire Terrier

Staffordshire Bull Terrier

Certain physical characteristics of mixed-breed dogs—a squarish-shaped head or a bulky body type—may lump these dogs under the same heading, and they will be forever referred to as Pit Bulls no matter how distant the connection may actually be.

Pit Bulls generally trace back to English bulldogs once bred to bait bears or bulls, meaning they were taught to latch onto the faces of these larger animals and "hold" them in place. Efforts gradually were made to combine the strength of a "bulldog" with the agility and gameness of the terrier, and this resulted in the evolutic of distinct breeds.

In 1835, when Great Britain eventually banned blood sports as being inhumane, many enthusiasts turned to dog fighting as a substitute—a sordid, violent practice, which, sadly, continues today, even though it's against the law and is *very* inhumane.

At the same time, Pit Bulls have become cherished for making wonderful family pets, service dogs, police dogs, therapy dogs, movie stars, and heroes in the rescues of many imperiled Humans. Unfortunately, Pit Bulls also are sometimes trained to become attack dogs, guarding narcotics operations and other unsavory and illegal activities.

Indiscriminate over-breeding has led to a huge surplus of stray Pit Bull types, along with other breeds. Without proper training, exercise, socialization and care, *any* stray dog can become a dangerous bully, just trying to stay alive. Pit Bulls are no exception. When stray dogs join packs and learn to become aggressive, the danger of unhappy interactions with Humans multiplies. No matter a dog's breeding, a severely abused or neglected dog can become a serious problem and a danger to Humans.

Since Pit Bulls do have a reputation as Fighting Dogs—whether or not they have ever *been* in a fight—they are often unreasonably feared and suffer from breed discrimination.

Laws now exist in many places that punish *all dogs* of certain breeds, whether they are Bad Dogs or not. Legislation is often aimed specifically at banning Pit Bulls—but this is slowly changing, as people realize exactly *who* is really at fault when someone gets hurt.

Bad Owners who neglect and abuse their animals, turning them into Bad or Dangerous Dogs—and then allow them to run loose off their leashes, are the ones who should be targeted and punished…and many communities are finally coming to realize this.

One of the most remarkable things about Pit Bulls is that so many former Fighting Dogs—once rescued from the short, brutal Life of a Fighting Dog—have gone on to become model citizens, beloved by their adoptive families. This is quite a testimony to their resilient, valiant natures. They really do want to please.

If you have enjoyed this story and want to learn more about Pit Bulls—or even adopt one—do your Homework. Learn everything you can about the breed, background and behavior of your prospective new family member.

Commit to providing the time and energy your new friend will require. If you haven't the time to give—or can't afford what will be needed—don't adopt a dog. *Any* dog.

Volunteer your time at an Animal Shelter or Rescue, instead. You will have lots of opportunity to enjoy canine companionship without having to commit to the long-term responsibility of owning a Dog.

Remember: When you adopt a Dog, it's like adopting a Child. You can't just ignore it when something else comes up. Your Dog will be making a lifetime commitment to *you*—and will be depending upon you to provide for its needs throughout its entire lifetime.

That's no small responsibility. But, in exchange, the rewards are *huge.*

The love and single-minded adoration of a Dog can change *your* Life.

Can we do no less than to live up to our Dog's good opinion of *us*?

Some Favorite Dog Quotes:

"I care not for a man's religion whose dog and cat are not the better for it."
~Abraham Lincoln

"A dog is the only thing on earth that loves you more than he loves himself."
~ Josh Billings

"The better I get to know men, the more I find myself loving dogs."
~ Charles de Gaulle

"One reason a dog can be such a comfort when you're feeling blue is that he doesn't try to find out why."
~Author Unknown

"The average dog is a nicer person than the average person."
~Andy Rooney

"If a dog will not come to you after having looked you in the face, you should go home and examine your conscience."
~Woodrow Wilson

"The greatest pleasure of a dog is that you may make a fool of yourself with him, and not only will he not scold you, but he will make a fool of himself, too."
~ Samuel Butler

"Dogs are better than human beings because they know but do not tell."
~ Emily Dickinson

"You think dogs will not be in heaven? I tell you, they will be there long before any of us."

~ Robert Louis Stevenson

Other books by Pam Daoust:

THE HONU WHO KNEW TOO MUCH,
A Fable For Grownups and Children

Ms. Daoust also writes historical romances and novellas under the pen name of Katharine Kincaid. Her titles available as eBooks include:

PAINTED HORSE

RIDE THE WIND

RACE THE DAWN

MASTER OF HORSES

WINDSONG

WILDWOOD

KINDLED FIRE

HOT TOMATO